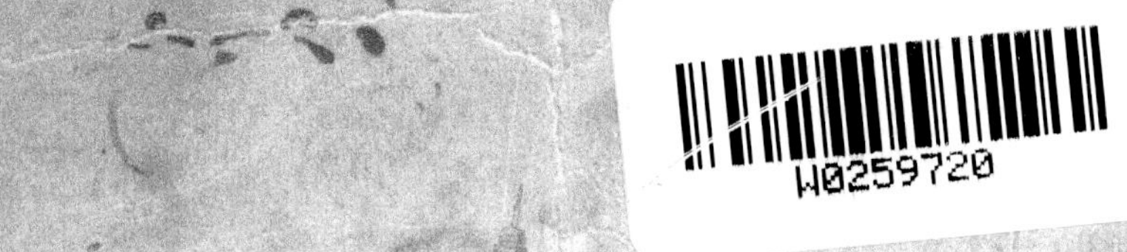

W0259720

ROAD TRIP TO LOVE

NYLLA CAMPHRY

Please feel free to send me an email. Just know that my publisher filters these emails. Good news is always welcome.

Nylla Camphry - nylla_camphry@awesomeauthors.org

Sign up for my blog for updates and freebies!
nylla-camphry.awesomeauthors.org

Copyright © 2015 by Nylla Camphry

All Rights reserved under International and Pan-American Copyright Conventions. By payment of required fees you have been granted the non-exclusive, non-transferable right to access and read the text of this book. No part of this text may be reproduced, transmitted, downloaded, decompiled, reverse-engineered or stored in or introduced into any information storage and retrieval system, in any form or by any means, whether electronic or mechanical, now known, hereinafter invented, without express written permission of BLVNP Inc. For more information contact BLVNP Inc. The publisher does not have any control over and does not assume any responsibility for author or third-party websites or their content. This book is a work of fiction. The characters, incidents and dialogue are drawn from the author's imagination and are not to be construed as real. While reference might be made to actual historical events or existing locations, the names, characters, places and incidents are either products of the author's imagination or are used fictitiously, and any resemblance to actual persons living or dead, business establishments, events or locales is entirely coincidental.

About the Publisher

BLVNP Incorporated, A Nevada Corporation, 340 S. Lemon #6200, Walnut CA 91789, info@blvnp.com / legal@blvnp.com

DISCLAIMER

This book is a work of FICTION. It is fiction and not to be confused with reality. Neither the author nor the publisher or its associates assume any responsibility for any loss, injury, death or legal consequences resulting from acting on the contents in this book. The author's opinions are not to be construed as the opinions of the publisher. The material in this book is for entertainment purposes ONLY. Enjoy.

Road Trip to Love

By: Nylla Camphry

ISBN: 978-1-68030-677-4
©NyllaCamphry2015

Table of Contents

To all those people
who don't believe in a happy ending for themselves...

Your lives are stories that you get to write.

You can end it whenever and wherever you want,
just don't give up until you find the perfect ending for yourself.

FREE DOWNLOAD

Know more about Dare and Blake by reading the FREE chapter when you sign up for the author's mailing list!

nylla-camphry.awesomeauthors.org

CHAPTER ONE

"Paris is overrated."

That sentence ended with me getting a pillow cushion thrown at my face.

At least it wasn't the book she had in her hand.

"It's the city of love, Dare. " Hayley said. "What more can you want?"

"If it was the city of anything else I might consider it." I replied.

"You and your anti-love attitude." Hayley sighed as she flipped through a book titled *What to Do in Paris When You Arrive*. I took a few steps back, hoping when she throws the book because of my next words, it would miss me.

"Honestly I'm just being rational. " I said "Love is simply a rush of a lot of hormones…"

She threw the book before I could complete my sentence but it missed me by a good two feet.

Thank God.

I mean getting hit by an eight-hundred-page book would leave a bruise. Yup, you heard me. Eight hundred pages of what to do in Paris and there was an entire chapter dedicated to foot massages.

Yes, it is as lame as it sounds.

"Come on, Dare." Hayley whined looking at me with her big brown eyes. "This is our last summer before college and we had made a pact ever since we were twelve that we would go on a road trip through the breathtaking European country side. So stop being a kill joy and choose a country."

I rolled my eyes, "It's not that easy. " I said. "I mean there are a lot of factors in—"

"You rejected Spain because you don't like salsa." She interrupted. "And I'm pretty sure salsa is from Mexico."

"It's not. " I retorted, hurt that she would ever question my knowledge when it came to food.

"I don't care. " Hayley said. "You are going to pick a country now and we are going to go there and have the time of our lives."

"But…" I said helplessly.

"I want to watch the new episode of Keeping Up with the Kardashians. I need to see if Khloe and Lamar make it, which means you have to pick right now."

I scan the desk in front of us which is covered with just about every Lonely Planet book on every possible country in Europe.

This is hopeless. Maybe we should just go to France.

But just then by some sort of miracle my eye lands on a Lonely Planet book on the ground which the both of us had failed to scan through.

It's perfect.

I turn the book around to show Hayley the title and she rewards me with a grin.

"Italy, here we come."

CHAPTER TWO

It should be every girl's dream: going on a summer road trip with your best friend through the gorgeous Italian countryside. Well, they forgot the best part. What happens when your best friend brings her boyfriend along?

Well, in that case, you could notify the Oxford Dictionary to change the definition of third wheel to Dare Williams.

"No, you are my teddy bear."

"No, you are."

"No, you are."

What did the poor teddy bear ever do?

What did I ever do to deserve this?

I mean sure I should be happy for Hayley and Dave. Yes, his name was just about as uncreative as he was and the fact that it could only be differentiated with mine because of one letter, did not put him high on my list of people who I would like to go on a road trip with.

It was hard trying to like him for several reasons but this… this was supposed to be a road trip for the two of us, Hayley and I. We were the ones who had been planning the trip since we were twelve years old, making playlists for the long rides in the car. But now it was the three of us: the happy couple and the disgruntled eighteen-year-old who was the definition of a loner.

I really didn't know what melted Hayley's heart. Dave was pretty average anyway. Considering the fact that Hayley grew up watching TV and reading books that featured boys that were too good to be true, I always thought Hayley would never settle for anyone, but instead be the one to try to find the perfection and once she saw how deluded she was and realize that finding anything any form of perfect in reality was next to impossible she would come live with me and we would be termed as the lonely old ladies with only cats to keep them company.

But that was okay with me, because at the end of the day I'd still have Hayley never mind the ungrateful cats.

Then came along Dave Dennings.

At first sight it was almost laughable as to how he could even hope to have Hayley Smithson. She had always been the girl with the perfect tan that matched her jet black hair and ridiculously long legs to give her a set of features that could easily be put on the cover of any magazine.

Dave Dennings on the other hand was simply… simple. There was nothing extraordinary in his nervous personality. There was nothing extraordinary about the fact that he couldn't hold up a two minute conversation with another person before totally spacing out.

No, Dave was nowhere near extraordinary, and yet of all the boys Hayley could have chosen, she chose to go out with him. She chose completely ordinary Dave and when it had first started I assumed that they wouldn't last for a week.

They had been dating for a few months now and Hayley claimed she was madly in love. I guess he was, too, but it was hard figuring out Dave behind his always blank expression. I had been looking forward to our trip, a totally Dave-free three weeks without me being the terribly grumpy third wheel to their Shakespearean-like romance.

I knew that made me a terrible friend but I needed my friend back. I needed my only friend back and the only way that would happen was if she got some time away from Dave.

But I was wrong because, coincidentally, Dave was going to Italy to meet his cousin.

Yes, I was shocked. Plain, old Dave had a wild cousin who was currently in Italy on a trip with his friends. So when Dave asked Hayley, she did the most expected thing of her and said yes after showering him with some sloppy kisses and voila our twosome became the very much in-love couple and me.

Yay.

We were in the immigration office in Rome with dozens of other people, mostly were Italians who were constantly arguing loudly. I did try my best to get a faint idea of what they were talking about in a desperate attempt to block out Dave and Hayley's "No, I love you more" dialogue.

I am here for the pizza. I said my mantra over and over again trying not to lose it.

When it was finally my turn at the immigration counter after a long fifteen-minute wait, I sighed in relief.

"Miss, what is your name." The guy in the counter said with a heavy Italian accent. He then threw a look behind my shoulder and immediately made a face. I didn't even have to turn around to figure out that Hayley and Dave had moved onto their making-out stage.

I gave the man behind the counter a look that said "I don't want to be here either."

"Darella Pam Williams." I flinched slightly as I said my full name, "US national."

He nodded clearly bored and said, "Do you have the form?"

I nodded and handed him my immigration form and he quickly looked over it, looking up only once to see if I looked similar to girl in the picture on my passport. He did a double take though, his eyes widening confused for a moment.

I didn't blame him really. That picture was one of the worst pictures ever taken in the history of photography. The girl in there had messy blonde hair that resembles grass and dull greyish green eyes that were unfocused which made her look like something out of a zombie movie.

The girl standing in front of him on the other hand actually looked like she was making an attempt. Her hair actually stayed in place, after hours of struggling with the straightening iron and the red dip-dyed streaks at the bottom actually gave her an edgier look.

He gave me another glance just to be sure and then stamped my passport and gestured me to move along.

I quickly walked off and craned my head to look for the two love birds. I took a step backward and someone subsequently crashed into me, knocking me down along with my heavy backpack.

"Shit!"

"Bloody Hell!"

I rub my head to see who had collided with me and I saw the hottest guy I had ever seen in my life.

No kidding.

He was blonde with an angular face and a jawline that made him the absolutely gorgeous and drool-worthy. He was young, about nineteen or twenty, and had the best cologne that my nose had ever had the opportunity to come across.

I judge people by smell, sue me.

I must have been staring for a really long time before he said, "Are you all right?"

Holy mother of god... he's British!

I quickly snapped out of my trance trying my hardest not to blush in front of him. I meant sure, our school had some boys who looked decent but this guy resembled something extremely close to the perfection I thought Hayley was deluding herself with during her pre-Dave era.

And he's British.

"You should really watch where you are going," he said rudely getting up and leaving me staring at him in shock at him from the floor.

You forgot the word jerk, Dare.

"Oh, well. I didn't think that I would have to look out for jerks who do not know the meaning of chivalry." I said pushing myself off the floor.

Of course he wouldn't be nice. It just didn't work like that. Hot guys who were genuinely nice could be easily compared to something like unicorns—a total myth.

He makes a disgusted face. "I am taught to be chivalrous to girls."

Wow, way to go Dare of all the people in the airport, you find a way to crash into the biggest jerk of all time.

Pay no attention to the fact that he may be the hottest, too, which was hard to do considering the fact that I couldn't get my mouth to close as I stared straight at him with zero shame.

I've been taught to be chivalrous girls. Seriously? Was that the best he could do?

I glared at him icily. "Have you perhaps been taught what girls are?"

He was stunned by my response, clearly not expecting me to backlash his comment. I didn't blame him to be honest, I did seem like the quiet shy types, which I was in reality.

But some people just got on my nerves.

"Whatever," he said. "I don't have time for this."

With that he simply brushed past me and walked away without a second glance.

How rude.

I slowly got up, picking myself up rather gingerly from the floor. I bend down to pick up my passport which had tumbled out of my hand when I notice a plain leather bound book lying near my feet.

"Hey, you left your…" I stopped as I realised that it was hopeless as he was long gone.

I pick up the book and give it a quick once-over. It is relatively blank except for a few phone numbers here and there along with the names of a few places in Italy. There is a name written on the first page with freakishly neat handwriting:

Blake Durham.

"Wow, Dare…" Hayley came from behind, grinning "…you manage to find the sexiest guy in the airport who just happens to be British. By the looks of him he's probably related to royalty. Maybe you shouldn't be so anti-love anymore."

"He happens to be a total jerk. " I said.

"They all are at first glance." Hayley said dismissively. "But that shouldn't stop you from taking a chance with someone."

And that was yet another side effect of the marvel that was Dave. Ever since Hayley started dating Dave she made it very clear that she felt extremely bad about making me the unwanted third wheel.

So she started setting me up. I obviously said no to all considering the fact that Hayley tried to set me up with a wide array of absolute strangers who I knew from first glance were going to be a disaster.

Blake Durham would certainly fall into that category due to his attitude problem.

"I don't even know him, Hayley. " I said. "Chances are we are never going to see each other again."

"If it's meant to be, it's meant to be. Don't worry though you'll find someone as special as Dave is to me."

I quite seriously doubt that, I think to myself but I didn't said it out loud so I settled for a classic roll of my eyes as we waited for Dave to come.

Hayley smiled as she greeted him and kissed him. Pretty soon as expected they were once again making out in front of me.

Oh, come on. It's not like he just came back from fighting a war.

Well, at least Dave was nice despite his dorkiness unlike certain British boys who got full marks for looks, but zero for personality.

Well, Blake Durham, I glanced at the leather book in my hand, *I hope we never meet again.*

And maybe somewhere deep inside even as I said those words, I knew that I would meet him again because without a moment's hesitation I slipped the book into my backpack.

CHAPTER THREE

"You are joking, aren't you?" I said looking at Hayley.

"Oh, come on, Dare," Hayley whined. "It makes sense."

"This is a road trip!" I exclaimed. "Our road trip. The one we, the two of us, have been planning since we were twelve. I cannot believe you are being so selfish."

"Dare…"

"You know what? Forget this," I said snatching the ticket from her hand. "I'll talk to you later."

With that I stalked off and disappeared into the cobbled streets of Rome.

This trip had been going fine.

Rome was beautiful and absolutely breathtaking in every way. It gave an old world charm like no other and just standing on its streets, I could feel the history of this place engulfing me. Even Hayley and Dave's lovey-dovey attitude didn't put me down… much.

There was their absolute need to take a selfie of themselves every two minutes in front of every single street or building which annoyed me to no extent but I let it slip because if I started to argue, Hayley would probably make me take their pictures instead.

I tried my best to be cheerful despite everything and gobbled my wonderful pizza as we saw the beautiful sites that met us at every corner. I was doing a stellar job of not letting the fact that I was practically invisible on this trip get to me until Hayley completely crossed the line.

"So Dave and I were thinking if we could take a train directly to Venice from here. It's supposed to be super romantic."

And to top it all off she was already ready with the tickets as if my opinion on the matter didn't even mattered the slightest.

So I did what I did best—run away from the problem.

I sat down on the park bench letting my purse fall onto the ground as I buried my head into my hands. My backpack was still on my shoulders as I bent down to bury my face into my hands. It gave me little comfort knowing that at least if nothing else, I had my backpack, filled with books that would never make me feel left out.

My mind swirls with thoughts and most of them are filled with anger, bitterness and jealousy. The fact that she didn't even consider my opinion hurt me a lot more than it made me angry.

We used to be best friends, the type who used to tell each other everything. She used to ask my opinion on everything, from the color of the dress she would wear to school to what TV show she should start watching.

She needed me, genuinely needed me and now… she had Dave.

And I was jealous.

I was jealous of my best friend and the fact that she had someone who loved her very, very much. It sounded stupid but it was true. I was totally jealous of the fact that Dave actually made her feel needed.

But if it was not the fact that I was completely and quite hypocritically jealous of their relationship, I was also jealous of Hayley's ability to trust someone so much and so instantly especially since I couldn't.

I really was a terrible friend.

I finally got up and reached for my purse to call Hayley and finally give in to her whim but my hand grasped only air.

Crap.

I checked everywhere as a sudden sense of panic overwhelmed me. My mobile, passport and the majority of my cash was in it except for the two hundred euro notes that I had kept in my backpack with my iPod.

Oh, god, I'm so stupid. I had just carelessly thrown my purse on the ground not even stopping to think that it may get stolen.

The train ticket!

Which station, what time, I knew nothing.

Come on Dare, think.

I stared helplessly at the ground trying my best not to cry. This was a nightmare. I was stranded in another country with no resources and no way to contact anyone. My passport was missing along with any identity proof so booking a train ticket was also out of question.

The *American Embassy!* That was my only way out of here. I quickly backed up as I was thinking about my course of action but I bumped into someone and tripped falling right on them.

"Bloody hell!"

"Shit!"

I looked up to see none other than the boy who I had crashed into the airport standing in front of me.

Blake Durham.

"I know you," he said, his eyes narrowing.

"Good to know." I said getting back on my feet trying to ignore the stinging pain in my hand.

"You are that girl who couldn't watch your step in the airport and made me lose the planner," he said, his voice full of accusation.

You are probably the only guy who I know who actually has a planner.

"Here you go." I said taking out the book from my backpack, which was ironic to be honest. I had lost my purse along with my most valuable possessions but I still had his planner tucked safely inside my backpack. "I tried giving it to airport security but they had other major issues to deal with, so I kept it."

He gave me a suspicious look and was about to take it when his phone rang making him curse.

He picked it up swiftly and gave me the universal sign to wait.

"Wait, Dave. Slow down." he said into the phone. "What the happened?"

My ears picked up the name and I was filled with hope but it crashed down like a wave against a giant rock with the tiny probability of it being the Dave I was looking for. I almost laughed at the ridiculousness of the fact that I wanted to see Dave for once.

"What do you mean you lost her?" Blake's voice rose slightly. "And I thought you guys were driving down to Venice."

Can this be?

"Excuse me?" I said waving my hands in front of Blake. "What's this guy's last name?"

"Shhh," he said, intently listening to the phone.

"But…" I said but I was interrupted again.

"I am in Rome right now. I can help, but seriously the girl sounds like a nutcase just stomping off like that."

"I do not." I huffed but he doesn't listen to me.

"What does she look like?"

"Brown eyes." He repeated.

"Blonde hair with red streaks at the bottom."

I waved my hands in front of him frantically but he ignored me once again.

"Not very tall," he said, sighing. "How do you expect me to find her…?"

He suddenly stopped and looked at me. I gave him my biggest fake smile possible and waved at him and his eyes widen.

"Actually that won't be a problem," he said into the phone. "She is standing in front of me."

CHAPTER FOUR

It was four hours later that I found myself in a bright red Mustang sitting next to Blake in the passenger seat.

"So Dave is your cousin," I said slowly recalling the conversation that I had with Dave on his cousin's phone.

Yes... super normal, uncreative American Dave had an extremely hot, British cousin named Blake.

Wow. That was a plot twist I did not see coming.

To be honest it was rather unrealistic, too.

In fact, it was far more unrealistic than me happening to bump into Dave's cousin of all the people in Rome.

"Yes," Blake said curtly, his accent thick, as he drove through Rome's outskirts.

So uncomfortable silence was going to be the theme of this road trip. It wasn't that I had an issue with that. Uncomfortable silence had been the theme of my entire life most of the time.

I sighed as I recall my conversation with Dave and Hayley on the phone as they explained how they had gotten aboard thinking that I was already there when I didn't pick up my phone. By the time they found out that I wasn't there, the train had already picked up speed and had left Rome and me far behind it.

When I explained my dilemma I could make out that Hayley was close to tears as she blamed the entire thing on herself. Part of me felt that she was right, but the other part of me knew that it had been my own carelessness and stubbornness that had ultimately made me land in this giant mess.

Dave and Hayley had half the mind of coming back, but then Blake gave a perfect solution: Why don't I hitch a ride with him to Venice as he was already going there. Plus he could take me to the American Embassy in Rome and sort out my passport problem.

At first I was shocked. I mean the two interactions the two of us had only consisted of glaring and abusing. Plus he clearly didn't like me and he offering to do something nice for me was jaw dropping. Dave must have thought that, too, because he dropped his phone causing the call to cut.

But true to his word, Blake had taken me to the American Embassy where I had explained my dilemma. The lady who I met looked like she had seen cases like this many times simply took a picture of me made me fill out a couple of forms and asked me to leave my parents' numbers with them so that she could verify my identity.

It was that simple. All I had to do was show the temporary card they had given me at the airport and everything would go smoothly from there.

Now as I was sitting in the car I was realizing that had been the easy part. The tough part would be spending five hours with an extremely moody British guy.

"Catch." I snapped out of my reverie as he threw a map at me.

"What?" I said, haphazardly catching it.

"I need you to tell me the directions," he said.

"Don't you have a GPS for that?" I asked. "Plus I have terrible road sense."

He simply rolled his eyes and said, "Be of some use. I have to take a detour because Dave couldn't manage you."

I would have argued but curiosity overpowered all my thoughts as I asked. "Where were you going anyway?"

I opened the map slowly and gave an encouraging nod hoping that he would consider it as a truce sign.

His hard eyes slowly softened as he said, "Amalfi, Pompeii and as much of Italy I can see. I find this country absolutely fascinating. With its beauty that literally take my breath away. I mean who needs Paris, the overrated city of love when you have this."

I found myself smiling at his choice of word. It was so typical me that I could have possibly mistaken it for something I had said.

"Why are you smiling?" he asked, looking at me curiously.

I simply shrugged and turned my attention to the large map that threatened to slip out of my hand and fly away.

Panic surged through me as I realized that in a few hours I would be back with Hayley and Dave.

Back to being a third wheel.

Maybe they would feel sorry for me and try to act more interested, but that would make it worse and it would ruin this entire trip even more. It would ruin my one and only chance to be happy before I go back, attend college, and live a future my parents planned for me.

"Are you all right?" Blake asked me, looking slightly weirded out. "You went from happy to depressed in two seconds flat."

"I'm fine." I said in a strangled voice.

He looked at me for a moment and I see concern flash through his face for just a moment but then it disappears almost immediately leaving him with his usual stony expression.

"There's an intersection coming up," he said with his voice back to its superior rude tone. "Which one should I take, right or left?"

I looked at the map and tried to pinpoint our location. I found it easily, almost too easily and looked at the two options ahead of me.

One led to Venice, the other went straight to southern Italy, leading us as far from Dave and Hayley as possible.

I was about to scan the maps and tell him the direction but at that very moment a strong wind came in and blew the map out of my hands.

I strained trying to reach the map that had been flattened against the backseat. I instantly regretted my decision to put on a seatbelt and not listen to Blake when he had laughed at my face and told me to stop being such a goody two shoes. I haughtily replied, "*Safety first.*"

I managed to reach it and settled down next to Blake who somehow managed to be completely oblivious to my mishap.

My eyes scanned the map again but I couldn't find the road anywhere.

"Which turn?" he asked and I started to panic.

"Umm..."

There was barely any distance left between the intersection and our car that was speeding towards it.

"Right." I said in panic and Blake took a sharp right that made me grip the car door tightly and squeeze my eyes shut.

"Don't worry," he said, looking at me presuming that I was car sick or something. "Only two more hours. It's a straight road from here."

I kept my mouth shut not telling him the fact that I may have lead him to the wrong direction.

It wasn't technically my fault. I had guessed that right must lead to Venice. Of course, I had chosen to go back to Hayley and Dave because it was the Dare thing to do.

It was the safe thing to do.

But now, despite my usually rational brain, every fiber of my body wanted it to be the wrong lane so that I could have my road trip.

Freedom lies in being bold, Robert Frost.

It was about time I became bold. It was about time I broke away from bonds that I set for myself. I didn't just want this road trip, I needed it.

But then there was the matter of Blake. We couldn't tolerate each other and our car journey had consisted of stony glances at each other and curt answers. I was willing to put up with him because I was used to a few rude comments and snobbish looks, but the real question was would he bear with me?

Well, I would find out in two hours.

It had been three hours.

The dim twilight was starting to set in. Up ahead city lights twinkled brightly and outshined the stars in the inky blue canvas of the sky that lay atop miles of beautiful vineyards that seemed to pave our way from Rome.

I was holding my breath and crossing my fingers like a little kid hoping to get a toy. With each passing minute after the intersection my hopes had been piling up like bricks but they had formed a skyscraper now. A precarious one, though. One that still needed cement to stay in place.

One that needed confirmation.

"It's curious." Blake had mentioned earlier. "According to what we had read earlier we should have been passing through Florence."

I recall as I had laughed nervously and clutched my seat hoping that he didn't suspect anything. No more than six hours since I had met in Rome, he had proved his relation with Dave by being just as absent minded as his American cousin.

It took about fifteen minutes for us to reach the town that we had been seeing in the horizon for a while now.

At first I couldn't register what I was seeing but I gasped loudly and even Blake looked awestruck.

It was a beautiful palace, its columns lit up with purple lights as it proudly stood above the glistening waterway which glowed bright green. Despite it being at a distance I could still see the enormity of the structure.

"The Royal Palace of Caserta." I mutter recalling the regal structure that was extremely admired in the pictures I had seen while researching for Italy.

I remembered wanting to go but when Hayley had said no because she wanted to go to Milan I had regrettably let it go along with Amalfi and Pompeii but now... Now I was sitting in the car just a few miles away from it.

"Why the hell are we in Caserta?" Blake stopped the car with a lurch and I broke out of my trance only to find Blake's cold grey eyes glaring at me for the umpteenth time today.

"Why are you blaming me?" I said despite knowing the fact that it was completely my fault. "I am not the genius who doesn't have a GPS and gives a girl who can't even tell you the route from her high school to her home, an extremely large and complicated map."

"Well, excuse me for thinking that you could be of use," he said. "Now you have led us to the complete opposite direction wasting approximately two days."

"But weren't you coming here anyway?" I yelled back. "It was written in your planner."

"You read my planner?" he said looking absolutely mad making me shrink back in my seat.

"Yes, but I didn't mean to," I said quickly. "It had happened by mistake."

Blake had gone awfully quiet and was just staring ahead with his knuckles white on the steering wheel. I didn't understand his sudden change in mood considering that his planner had next to nothing written in it, just the names of few place in Italy and the name Jenna.

"Let's just go get a hotel and we will leave for Venice first thing in the morning," he said starting the car again looking stoic and awfully calm.

My mind started to spin and once again I started to panic and I couldn't stop myself as I blurted out. "No!"

He looked at me his gaze hard but now it had a curious edge to it.

"Pleas," I said slowly. "I can't go back with them. This is my last chance to be free but if I go back I'll be stuck as the third wheel and my entire holiday will be ruined. Please this my last chance before college before my par—"

I broke off breathing heavily not able to believe that I just let loose so much to a complete stranger.

I couldn't see his face as he drove ahead. He just said in a monotone voice, "Let's just get a hotel for now."

And the skyscraper of hope came crashing down.

CHAPTER FIVE

The next day I dejectedly sat in the car with my backpack on my lap.

Despite my purse being stolen, I still had all my clothes, which I had retrieved from my hotel room in Rome. Well, it wasn't much but it was something to be happy about. I mean it could have been worse if all my clothes had been stolen and I was stuck with the same clothes.

And then if it rained…

Well then, Blake would have quite definitely left me on the side of the street pretending that he didn't know me and I was just some homeless groupie. I would certainly look the part, I was sure.

My situation was not that bad. I meant sure Blake had an attitude but it wasn't his fault I was a nosy bum.

Plus he was extremely easy on the eyes.

After we checked into a hotel Blake had become a true gentleman and had slept on the couch in the room and insisted that he paid for the room. I wouldn't have been that much help considering the fact that I only had two hundred euros with me and I still hadn't plucked the courage to call my parents and explain the situation.

The next morning, sheer disappointment washed over me and the very thought of going back and seeing Dave and Hayley all lovey-dovey was enough to make me want to hide under my covers and never come back out.

It wasn't that I had a problem with them. It was that I was completely and totally *jealous* of them.

It was pathetic, I know, but this trip was to give me a break from all of this. Seeing Dave and Hayley in love just rubbed it in my face that I would never get a shot at it thanks to my parents.

Blake was in the reception as I sat in the car and mulled over my broken hopes that were like once bright stars that were being sucked into a giant black hole of despair.

Yeah, I really didn't want to go back.

I was still lost in thought when Blake came and sat inside the car and offered me his cellphone.

"I think it's your mum. Dave must have given her my number," he said. "She wants to talk to you."

I froze. I could feel the colour draining out of my face as I reached for his phone, my hands shaking.

I grabbed the phone and for a moment I just stared at it unable to bring it closer to my ears.

"Are you all right?" Blake asked and I managed to nod tightly before opening the door of the car and stepping out.

"Hello." I said unsurely.

"Darella."

My mother's voice was clipped and cool without a hint of emotion. She said my name with no warmth, just acknowledgement.

"Yes, it's me, mother."

There was a pause.

"Your utter lack of irresponsibility never fails to surprise me. You're eighteen and you couldn't keep that head of yours focused for long enough to take care of your valuables. Oh, Darella, must you always remain such a stupid little girl?"

Her words stung but what hurt more was that I actually hoped that this time she would have an ounce of sympathy for me.

"I'm sorry." I said quietly. "You're right, I should have been smarter."

"What are you planning to do now?" She asked. "I hope you plan on coming back instantly rather than continue this foolish holiday of yours. I had already warned you about this silly vacation of yours."

"Yes, mother. I'll try my best to book the next flight out of here, although most of them are full."

"I'll send the jet if I have to," she said firmly "I can't have you around that airhead friend of yours for much longer. I've never liked her and she's always been a bad influence on you."

I didn't respond.

"And this boy you're currently with, I'm less than happy about this situation Darella. David Denning's cousin or not…"

"It's just for a day mom," I interrupted. "We are driving to Venice today to meet up with Hayley and Dave. That's it."

"Hmm."

I could almost see her expression, her red lips pursed and her eyes narrowed.

"I need to go, mom. " I said. "It's a long drive."

"All right. Oh, and Darella?"

"Yes?"

There was a small pause at the end of the phone and I, for just one second, I let myself hope that she would say something like, *I'm glad you're okay* or maybe a simple *I love you.*

"I'm very disappointed in you," she said and then she promptly cut the call.

I stood there, phone in hand, trying my best to fight the tears that threatened to fall.

No, I'm not going to cry, I told myself, *I am not going to cry.*

I then head back to the car making sure to keep my eyes on the ground through the entire process of opening the door and climbing back in.

"Tha—" My voice came out choked so I quickly cleared my throat and got a hold of myself and stretched out my hand with his phone. "Thank you."

When he didn't take it, I forced myself look up at him and he was staring at me curiously, his eyebrows scrunched up.

"Your p-phone." I stammered under his gaze. He blinked breaking eye contact and pocket his phone.

"You're welcome."

And then we were back to the usual awkward silence.

He started the car and I drifted off, thinking about my conversation with my mother. In fact, I only snapped out of my trance when he stopped the car in front of the majestic palace we had seen yesterday.

"What the…?" I began to say, highly confused looking at Blake who was getting out of the car currently.

I hastily followed him out of the car. For the first time since yesterday afternoon, I got a good look at Blake who looked like a model in his tight black t-shirt. He looked really good. His abs even put the statues of the Greek gods to shame and that was saying something.

Well, Dare, you cannot deny the fact that when it comes to fact that out of all the people you could have been stranded with Blake was probably the best anyone could get.

"We were here so might as well finish sightseeing," he said looking at me through his dark Ray Ban glasses. I couldn't quite read his gaze from behind his sunglasses, but I nodded almost too happily and followed him as he headed towards the ticket counter.

I did argue with him after all I did have some money but he simply said, "I'm British, not American, hence I actually know the word chivalry."

Well I couldn't say no after he pulled the chivalry card on me now could I?

Whatever was said and done, it was fun. It took us about an hour to see everything including the part where I almost fell in the waterway and Blake caught me in the last moment and ended up falling on the ground with me on top of him, grumbling something about me having absolutely no hand-leg coordination.

But it was fun.

After the entire incident with my purse getting stolen, I didn't think I would utter the word fun but thanks to Blake who surprisingly knew a lot about the palace acted as my unofficial tour guide, I got a taste of the holiday I wanted.

And to be honest that was the best I could ask for.

But like everything good, it came to an end and I found myself back in his car speeding away from the beautiful town.

"Thank you." I said smiling looking at Blake whose eyes were focused on the road.

He simply grunted and I let myself smile, tucking my head into a comfortable position as I put on my earphones and blasted music through them.

Despite Blake's macho appearance he was extremely nice. Nothing had forced him to take me the nosy little prick who got herself lost, to the palace but he did. I never did expect him to agree to the proposition that I had placed in front of him, after all to him I practically a stranger to him who he got stuck with, because of his cousin.

I didn't know when I fell asleep but it happened eventually as my mind slowly shut down in tune to beat of the song that was currently playing.

I woke up to ACDC.

Trust me their songs were brilliant but waking up just as they started the chorus to Highway to Hell was enough to give anyone a headache.

I ripped the cords of the earphones out of my ears just in time for me to make sure that I wouldn't be permanently deaf.

"That was brutal." I grumbled, rubbing my ears.

Beside me, Blake chuckled. "Do you know that you talk in your sleep?"

My mouth fell open.

"W-what did I say?" I stammered.

"Nothing really." He replied with an amused smile, "You were just mumbling."

I sighed in relief.

"But I do believe it was something in the lines of it's not fair that all the British guys get all the good looks plus the husky voice."

I groaned and he laughed and suddenly I was aware of how quickly the tension between us vanished.

"So how long till we meet your dear cousin?" I said tying my hair as the wind whipped mercilessly against my face.

We were currently climbing up a mountain from what I could gather. The sharp craggy rocks rose up on both sides all mighty and proud.

"Well, that maybe a problem," he said slowly grinning.

I raised an eyebrow but before I could reply we take a sharp turn and I was met with one of the most beautiful sights known to man.

The deep blue sea stretched far and wide below the road. The cliff face ended in jagged rocks where waves competed for dominance as they crashed with each other, thundering and roaring.

It was blue. So blue.

"It's beautiful, isn't it?" he said and all I could do was grin.

"B-but…" My mouth failed to say the words but he grinned understanding what I was trying to say.

"Welcome to Amalfi, Dare."

CHAPTER SIX

"So, Blake. It's your turn now."

"Turn for what?" Blake replied as he messily licked his ice cream, leaving some on the tip of his nose.

"To choose where to go." I said wiping the ice cream of his nose with my index finger and tasting it. He made a disgusted face and inched away from me whilst rolling his eyes.

"Damn. I should have taken hazelnut." I sighed wistfully. "But you have to choose where to go. I already did."

Despite getting off to a rocky start we found out that we got along extremely well. We had the same taste in music and art. Overall, I was having a good time.

It was impossible not to, if I was being completely honest.

Yesterday when we arrived I was absolutely ecstatic. I barely knew Blake but I hugged him at least eight times and I wasn't a person who was comfortable with displays of affection. What Blake had done for me, no one ever had. No one ever would. To everyone else I was a snobbish rich girl who was Miss Goody-Two-Shoes and the most daring thing I had ever done was dip dye my hair.

But Blake didn't judge me by my name. He didn't judge me by my parents. He judged me by me and granted that he found me annoying and irritating at times, he liked me enough to take me with him. That is more than I could say with anyone else.

So we had spent the night a hotel room after eating dinner on the beach. I called Hayley too and begged her to cover for me with my mom. She was all too happy and agreed instantly and we decided that if my mom decided to call either of us we would just lie and say that we were all together and Blake had joined our group.

I couldn't see my mom being too happy about it but I didn't care. I wanted this and more importantly I needed this.

From what I observed Blake was pretty much loaded, maybe even as rich as my parents were. You could see it in his taste of food, cars, hotels and his clothes. But I didn't ask him after all I had done enough prying with his planner.

"The tour was brilliant, admit it." I said.

"You shall get no such confession out of me," he said getting up and offering me a hand which I promptly take to lift myself up the large step. "It was boring. All we did was go to a cathedral and see a beach from far. I thought you were more exciting than this, Dare."

"I am." I whined.

"Well, I am going to show you what the real Amalfi is all about," he said and started walking ahead weaving skillfully through the dense crowd.

I took back everything nice I said about him. He was rude, arrogant… and downright rude.

I was not boring. I was adventurous and the clear proof was the fact that I was right now with him and not with Hayley. I tried to ignore the fact that I was here only because of a mistake that I had not intended to make.

I was not boring and I would prove it to him.

"Are you crazy?" I yelled hoping that he could hear me above the thunderous crashing of the waves on the rocks.

"I'm not telling you to jump," he said calmly. "Just sit."

He pointed to the giant rock in front of us. If we sat on it then our toes would just about touch the frothing sea water. I didn't know how he knew about this place that was tucked away behind the southern beach completely covered with giant mountainous cliffs on either side. It had been a long hard trek but I hadn't complained even once hoping to dismiss his opinion of me being boring.

But I had reached my limit, so as Blake made his way to the rock and sat he just glanced behind and shook his head and muttered "Typical."

That's just about when I lost it.

I was a quiet girl. I always followed the rules, kept in line never questioned anything. With Hayley I was different. I was sarcastic, brave and bolder which is why despite us being polar opposites I had stuck with Hayley for so long.

Needless to say we didn't match. She took me for granted most of the times unwittingly and I let her. It wasn't because I was very attached to her. It was because I was scared that if I lost her, I would lose myself. I would lose my sarcastic, brave, bold self and be left with a shell of a girl that I was around everyone else.

But when Blake muttered that one little word something in me snapped and I did something I never thought I would do.

I shook my shoes off and took of my T-shirt which left me only in my camisole. I then in turn took my skirt off and was left in a pair of dark cotton shorts I had worn underneath.

Then I jumped.

I cannonballed straight into the frothing Mediterranean ocean and sunk into its deep embrace. I didn't know how long I was underwater but I could no longer hear the waves and it was completely peaceful. The sunlight wove its way through the water looking like fragile curtains of lights and for once I was alone by choice and I liked it.

I thrust myself upward, accepting the fact that I had to join the world of humans again and with one last push my head broke above the surface leaving behind the secret sanctuary of peace right underneath me.

"Are you crazy?" Blake yelled, now standing on top of the rock, the lines on his face etched with worry.

"No, I'm boring." I said as I struggle against the current that pushed me against the rock but I was still grinning. The freedom of the sea was spectacular and for the first time in a long time I felt free, too.

"You could die." He deadpanned.

"I'm alive aren't I?" I said enjoying. "Now stop being a wuss and jump in."

He raised an eyebrow. "I like living."

"And you call me boring."

"Okay! That may have been wrong." He yelled out. "I meant bat-shit crazy."

"Chicken."

"Cuckoo."

"I think you just laid an egg."

"Oh, get over yourself," he said, rolling his eyes.

"I will once you get in."

With that I took a deep breath and sunk underwater constantly moving my hands to fight against the current. It wasn't as fast as it looked, it was simply a small string that constantly tugged on you gently. The only disturbance in the otherwise quiet world.

A giant splash drove me back and I broke out on the surface to find Blake trying to float. He was waving his hand with no coordination and trying his best to keep his head above the water.

He can't swim. Well, at least not well.

I quickly swam forward towards him and yelled over the waves. "Calm down, Blake."

He became even more frantic and I swam forward blinded by his splashing but at the last moment I managed to find his hands and forced them to stop and grab my waist. He looked startled but followed me and calmed down.

I had always been a strong swimmer and supporting the both of us, although tiring, wasn't too hard for me. He was much bigger than me which made it harder but I managed.

"See? I told you it was a bad idea," he said.

"Well, who knew you couldn't swim," I said laughing and just how dorky and troubled this version of Blake looked as compared to his usual calm and composed self. "Simply move your legs in a circular motion and don't let go of me."

"Not bloody likely," he said trying his best to follow my instructions.

"And you call me batshit crazy." I smiled and he rolled his eyes but his grip on my waist tightens.

"I want to show you something," I said. "Take a deep breath."

His grey eyes widened. "W-what?"

I slowly went down and he pulled himself closer to me and I take a deep breath and went underwater.

The first thing I noticed was how close he was and the fact that his eyes were tightly shut.

That's a pity, he does have the most beautiful grey eyes.

I put my hand over his eyelids and slowly raised them revealing his brilliant grey eyes. He looked different underwater. His dark blonde hair looking pale and his usually tanned skin now matching my complexion on the paler side.

His eyes were different, too, unguarded, curious and most of all in awe, as if he couldn't believe what he was seeing. He looked... human. Not a rude arrogant boy with good looks to put a god in shame who always puts up a wall.

I pointed down and showed him the school of bright, yellow fish that pass below us at some depth. He smiled and I saw just how genuine it was and returned his smile. He then looked up admiring the thin beads of light that pass through the ever changing water.

I slowly pushed us up and he tried his best, too, and pretty soon we gasped for oxygen a required necessity that we deprived our lungs for so long. He didn't talk as I slowly led us to a rock and he hoisted himself up easily being back on land. He grabbed me just as easily and pulled me up and I let out and involuntary shiver.

We both changed quickly, sat on the rock and watched the sun slowly make its way to the sea. We sat in comfortable silence enjoying the beat of waves.

Blake was the first to break the silence.

"Times like these make you believe in a higher power."

I nodded.

"Living in a city for all my life I never realized that all of this existed, much less I would get too see it with my own eyes." I replied softly my eyes fixated on the canvas of red, purple and orange that stretches before me.

"Dare?"

I tore my gaze and found myself looking at Blake's eyes again.

"Huh?" I said incoherently.

"Remind me never to call you boring again."

CHAPTER SEVEN

"This place gives me the creeps." I said. "It's fascinating and all, no doubt about that but extremely creepy."

"Oh, come on." Blake whispered sarcastically inside the dark room. "What's creepy about some guy who looks like he has seen Medusa?"

I let out an involuntary shiver as I saw a statue in front of me almost disintegrating. But what was creepy was that it was an actual person from Pompeii doing god know what when Mount Vesuvius decided to blow up leaving him in stone forever.

"Every block of stone has a statue inside it and it is the task of the sculptor to discover it." Blake said quoting one of Michelangelo's famous sayings.

"How ironically accurate," he muttered, sighing and walking ahead trying to keep up with the group ahead.

"We are terrible people," I said, trying to keep up with Blake and the tour guide who walked just as fast as she talked. "We are making fun of a guy who died thousands of years ago with no fault of his own. For all you know that the poor guy must have really needed to pee but never got the chance, too."

Blake stopped midway making me crash into him.

"I don't get you."

I rolled my eyes and said, "You are not supposed to. I am supposed to be the mysterious, beautiful girl."

"Yes," Blake said dryly. "Who has absolutely no grace?"

As if to prove his point I tripped and crashed into the person ahead of me.

"Okay!" I huffed. "Not everyone can have the godlike grace that you walk with and seriously, are you on steroids?"

"You know forget I said it," he said. "For all I know that you are going to try and balance on top of Mount Vesuvius to show just how graceful you are."

"Now that you mention it…" I trailed off.

"You are absolutely and completely frustrating, Darella Williams," he said.

"Do not call me that," I said. "Please just use, Dare."

"Why not?" His mouth transformed into one of his famous smirks. "Darella Williams."

"Because you sound like my parents," I deadpanned and walked ahead my mood clearly sour.

"Hey, wait up," he said. "I'm sorry, I really didn't know that this would affect you so much."

"Right," I said curtly and walked faster, trying to tune out my thoughts along with Blake's voice and did my best to concentrate on the tour guides fascinated talk about people who burned alive.

"Peace offering," Blake stated as he shoved an ice cream underneath my nose.

"We are not at war," I replied and went back to reading the book about Pompeii and chugging on water so that I was well prepared for the trek up Mount Vesuvius.

"Could have fooled me, Dare," he said.

I looked up at him and stared at his genuine grey eyes that were once again steely and guarded but much more open and softer than when I first met him. I shook my head and took the ice cream from him realising what a drama queen I was being.

He just called you by your full name Dare, that doesn't make him your parents. He would have to enroll you in business school and try to marry you off to another guy for the company's benefit to earn that precious title.

"Hazelnut," I murmured, surprised.

"Yeah, you wanted it yesterday," he said, looking slightly confused.

"Yes, I did," I said, surprise clear in my tone, "I didn't think you would remember."

He simply smiled. "Well hopefully this time you will refrain from licking it off my nose."

I scooped some of the ice cream on my finger and smeared it on his nose. "You wish."

He laughed and smeared some of his ice cream on my cheeks and pretty soon we are covered in ice cream.

"That was real mature of us," he said, wiping off the gooey mess on his face.

"True," I said, sarcasm heavily dripping from my tone. "We totally were not behaving like five-year-olds."

We stared seriously at each other before we burst out laughing again. People were staring at the both of us but I honestly couldn't care less because at that moment I was happy at that moment and for some reason the main reason was Blake Durham.

The guy who I had labeled as an arrogant jerk in the airport but in the end had turned out to be a dork who couldn't swim and had a bigger heart than anyone I had ever met. For some reason a guy who was so completely different from me gets me the most.

I always found the idea of love or even attraction funny. I had never felt it before and my parents had ensured that I would most probably never feel it either. But sitting on a park bench in Pompeii, Italy far away from home across a boy, I never knew existed until a few days back I knew without a doubt that the butterflies in my stomach and the increasing speed of my heart every time I glanced at him that I had a massive thing for Blake Durham.

CHAPTER EIGHT

"This may sound extremely rude and blunt…" Blake informed me as we speed towards Florence through the beautiful Naples countryside. "…but why are you afraid of your parents?"

I blinked at his question, my good mood going down the drain. I should have expected it really after the phone call but I was hoping he would drop it.

"You don't need to answer the question if you don't want to." He said quickly when he sees my lips are in a straight line and I was reluctant to answer.

I was actually enjoying myself yesterday until Blake's phone rang. I was fooling around, a luxury I didn't get too often back home. I was even obliviously happy and made fun of Blake's Spice Girls ringtone. He had given me a sour look before answering the phone.

My mother probably said one line to Blake at the most but it was enough to make his scowl deepen. When he handed the phone to me, I expected it to be Hayley or Dave but the minute I put it to my ear I knew it wasn't either of them.

You see, I had experienced that parents were supposed to be warm and compassionate to their children but unfortunately I had never experienced it first-hand. My parents were workaholics who liked to immerse themselves in their work, and if they ever glanced my way it would be just to correct something. I wasn't afraid of them. I just didn't know how to stand up to them, how to tell them that I didn't want to follow the path they had put out for me.

So when I put my ear to the phone I felt a sense of dread I always related to my parents, especially my mother. The conversation went on for quite some time. Even longer than last time and far more brutal because my mother figured out I was lying.

Hayley must have cracked and my mother was absolutely furious, to say the least, throughout the conversation. It wasn't a conversation as much a one-sided lecture. By the time I put the phone down, I was physically and mentally exhausted and tears fought their way up to my eyes.

But I didn't cry. I didn't let out a single sob or even the tiniest bit of a tear drop afraid because every time my mother's warnings and threats rang through my head somehow looking at Blake's intense and worried gaze on me calmed me down. It made me braver, stronger and much more determined not to show weakness.

But the one silver lining in our entire conversation was that no matter how much power the Williams name had, even she couldn't get me on an earlier flight because everything was booked and the jet wasn't big enough to make such a long journey instantly and would at least take a week to prep.

And that just made me far more determined to go through with this.

I tried my best to remain normal after I kept the phone down, but my sudden silence spoke to him louder than anything I could have possibly told him

"I don't know where to start to answer that question," I said softly cutting though the silence that had settled thickly around us.

The air whipped around us as the car sped past the vineyards which looked like a blur of green against the blue background.

He stopped the car suddenly and I was thrown forward.

"Ow," I muttered rubbing my head. "What was that for?"

He turned the key trying to start the car but the car just sputtered and died.

"The car just died on me." He muttered pressing his foot on the accelerator hard.

"Great." I muttered getting out of the car. I sighed dejectedly as Blake followed me out of the car.

"Now what?" I asked.

He tapped on his phone rapidly and then held the screen in front of me and said, "There is a rest house somewhere near here, we will have to walk it."

"Oh, ok." I said. "Lead the way."

"Holy crap." I said, gape mouthed.

"I know right it's amazing." He breathed and I couldn't help nodding to that.

We were standing in front of a glistening lake that was surrounded by vineyards all around.

"Tell me why stuff like this couldn't exist in the real world?" I asked my voice somewhere in between a whisper and a whine.

He raised his eyebrows curiously. "What do you mean real world?"

"Not this. Not this fantasy that's going to end the minute I go home to face reality." I said. "Not this dream I'm currently living in in which I have a shot at being happy."

My voice trailed off at his intense gaze.

"I think everyone has a shot at being happy Dare," he said. "Maybe not in the way they expect but in some way none the less."

"I have never been a part of everyone."

He lapsed into silence closing his eyes as if taking in the scratching of the leaves and the sweet and sour smell of the grapes.

"I knew a girl once…" he said "…she was like you. Beautiful, quietly loud, but brave. She taught me that we all had to be happy no matter what life threw at us because otherwise we would never really live, just exist like shells of what we could be."

My mind flickered back to the name of the girl written on his book but I kept quiet.

"It's a myth that bad things only happen to bad people, Dare, but when it happens to good people you have to take it with a smile," he said his stormy grey eyes looking like the sea on a stormy day. Dangerous, unpredictable and on the verge of lashing out. Yet it had a kind of soft edge to it.

"Like Robert Frost said, the best way in life is through."

I closed my eyes taking his words into account soaking it in trying to breathe in only the sweetness of the grapes around us and ignoring the sourness. Life was like grapes, sweet and sour. The best you could do was bite into one and hopefully it would turn out sweet.

The silence was defeating yet calming, somewhere in between Blake's hand had found mine and his fingers were curled around mine in a reassuring way like his words had almost.

"Thank you." I whispered softly. And I hoped he understood just how much I needed that and just how much it helped.

We made our way back to car after that hoping to get it started. We didn't speak much really but our actions and gestures were enough to convey what we were thinking.

The car started easily as we sat in it and as we sped through the vineyard I realised that the car had not stopped working after all.

CHAPTER NINE

"My father's name is Darren." I said softly with my eyes tightly shut that night in our hotel room.

"Huh?" I could hear Blake's confused voice which caused me to open my eyes and saw him peering curiously at me from the couch which he had insisted on taking.

"I think that's how you start a personal conversation." I said treading carefully.

"Oh," he said looking surprised but quickly recovers. "My father's name is James."

We both lapsed into an awkward silence where neither of us know what to say.

"Okay, this just a shot in the dark, but I think that you have to say something to continue the conversation."

"Rainbow Unicorn Poop?" I offered immaturely which made both of us laugh.

"Good try but it should be something like 'I'm Darella Williams' but I don't like being called that. I like the name Dare because it describes me perfectly with my brave and outlandishly daring personality."

My mouth dropped.

"What?" Blake asked. "It was the use of 'outlandishly' that ruined it, right? I knew…"

"You think I'm brave?"

The words tumbled out of my mouth and it sounds so unbelievable when it's being use do describe me."

"Remind again who jumped into the Mediterranean just for the hell of it?"

"I would call that stupid not brave." I stated.

"Nope, that's what you call brave, what was stupid was the boy who jumped into the ocean without knowing how to swim," he said chuckling. "All because a girl was calling him a chicken."

I laughed with him.

"And let's not forget the trek up Mount Vesuvius. What is your secret?" he asked. "You were easily going up the ledges despite your pathetic sense of balance. I, on the other hand, am not ashamed to say that I was literally shitting my pants. I questioned my manhood more times than I care to admit."

I quirked an eyebrow. "Your manhood? Really? You're afraid of heights and can't swim for peanuts anything else I should be warned about?"

"Yes, the fact that I have a ruggedly charming personality," he said, and I find myself rolling my eyes.

"Yes, your ruggedly charming personality was what was on display when you leaped into the Mediterranean and almost drowned like an idiot."

"In my defense it looked fun," he said innocently shrugging like a two-year-old. "On a completely different note, your mom seems like a hoot and a half."

Sarcasm dripped from every word but I didn't mind. He was the first person ever to face the side of my mother only I saw. The strict disciplinarian whose top priority was her image.

"Yup she is a hoot and a half. And it gets even better when you are face to face."

Blake shuddered. "I'm happy right here."

"So am I." I nodded in agreement. "Because what's waiting back for me is hell."

"Waiting back in Venice or in America?" He asked it casually but it really got me thinking.

"Both." I said after a while.

We stayed quiet for some time.

"Dave is a nice guy you know." Blake said earnestly. "Boring, but nice."

I quirked an eyebrow. "You don't have to sell your cousin to me really, Hayley has already done that."

"And has that changed your opinion about him by even the slightest?" He asked and I find myself shaking my head.

"Not really, no." I sighed. "I've been told I'm very judgmental."

"Judgmental, how?" He asked looking genuinely surprised.

"Well, I draw conclusions too fast. First impression is my only impression of the person really." I stated being honest.

"So, do you still think of me as the jerk who crashed into you in the airport and threw a diva fit just for kicks?" He asked sincerely and I cracked a smile as he said "diva fit."

"Well, *no.*" I admitted. "Not really."

"Then your entire theory of you being judgmental is wrong, you didn't judge me now did you?" he said.

"Yeah, well, you seem to be an exception to my rules. I meaning would have never ever gone on a road trip with a complete stranger, much less share a hotel room or anything."

"But you are doing it now, aren't you?" he said. "And it doesn't seem scary, does it?"

"Yeah." I said. "But honestly I feel I kinda forced the both of us in this situation especially you, almost against your will by reading the map wrong. I mean you did nothing to deserve getting stuck babysitting me."

"Hey I chose to go to Amalfi with you now didn't I?" he said. "And I really don't mind you're quirky sure but you're fun to be around. At least most of the time."

I raised an eyebrow. "Most of the time?"

"Need I remind you of the fact that in the hotel in Amalfi you got absolutely and totally drunk on alcohol so much so that you were fumbling to pronounce you're simple two syllable name?"

"What?" I shrieked. "I don't remember a thing really."

"Well Dare trust me sober you with no balance is still better than drunk you with even less balance," he said.

I blushed in embarrassment. "Oh, my god. I'm so sorry."

"Yeah, well, I didn't mind at the end of it," he said. "And as for you thinking that you forced yourself into this, I think you're wrong."

"What do you mean?" I asked.

"Dare, think back really hard. Are you telling me that you don't remember which way it was?"

I did as he said and the map flashes in front of my eyes the direction directly stated on it.

He was right, somewhere in the back of my mind I did know the way.

"I really didn't mean to purposely do it…"

"It's okay, Dare," he said gently. "But my point is that you never forced yourself into this. You were always ready to have this adventure, ready to step out of your comfort zone. Ready to live your life in your terms. And right now I'm telling you that you are ready. You just have to accept the fact that you don't have to feel guilty for wanting your own life and wanting to do it your way."

I stayed quiet for some time processing his words.

"You're telling me to start being courageous and brave," I said finally.

"You are brave, Dare, and according to Ernest Hemingway courage is simply grace under pressure. Despite your lack of balance I assure you have plenty of both. It's just time you accept it."

And even after he went to sleep, my eyes stayed open replaying this conversation over and over again.

CHAPTER TEN

The next morning we were back in Rome.

"Wow Rome is so pretty." I stated.

"Weren't you here before?" He asked and I give a nod.

"Yes, I was, but it looks so much better when you don't have to be the assigned photographer for the mushiest couple in the world." I said. "I mean, 'Ooh, let's take a picture near the gelato shop', Ooh let's take a picture of the pizza we ate', 'let's share a pizza and make Dare take the picture of us'."

Blake laughed. "Your friend seems like a piece of work."

I rolled my eyes. "Two out of the three examples were your cousin."

"Hey, we don't choose the family we are born into." He then added a little darkly. "Trust me."

Boy, do I know that.

"Well, you only have a lame cousin, who is obsessed with himself and food. I on the other hand have parents who are willing to marry me off to some complete stranger like a business deal."

I said it so nonchalantly that he didn't understand it at first. "Yeah I kn— Wait, what?"

His expression was one of total confusion and bafflement so much so that he looked absolutely adorable.

"Yup, pretty much." I said. "I've met the guy like two times and he is a total snob."

"Your parents are forcing you to marry someone?" The very idea sounds ridiculous to him, in fact it sounded ridiculous to mè, too.

"Yup, pretty much. After four years in Yale, I'm expected to get married to him immediately and be by his side or some crap like that I don't even know."

"And you're going to let them do it?" he said, sounding surprised. "You're engaged?"

I shrugged.

His looked horrified. "That's absolutely monstrous."

I laughed at his choice of words.

"Monstrous?" I asked him jokingly but he seemed to find nothing even remotely funny.

"How can you just let them do that to you?"

"I don't think I have a choice Blake." I said lightly trying not to show how much this conversation was taking a toll on me. "This is supposed to be my summer off, it's a miracle my parents agreed to this really."

"But that's crazy, you're eighteen, Dare," he said. "You're supposed to making bad choices, falling in love and living life and not putting a timer to your happiness."

I gave him a sad smile. "You're the exception, to the rule Blake. I'm not brave. I'm just plain me back home."

He looked at me like he couldn't believe what I was saying. I smiled at his expression.

"Blake you look like you're going to have an aneurism…"

"And you're not?" He burst out. "This is seriously ridiculous. I mean, you… you can't get… get married. You're eighteen!"

"Blake." I looked at him square in the eye, putting my hands on his shoulder. "Calm down."

Blake looked like he wanted to say a lot more but just then his phone started to ring.

"Aren't you going to pick that up?" I asked him and he rolled his eyes before saying, "We are not done."

"Pick up the phone." I said.

"No."

"Yes."

"Make me."

I rolled my eyes and he sighed in defeat taking it out of his pocket.

He smirked as he looked at his phone. "Oh, what do you know? It's your mother."

At first I couldn't decide what he was trying to convey but the second he picked up the phone and said in a sickly sweet voice. "Hello Mrs. Williams. Yes, she is here…"

"Blake." I hissed standing in front of him. "Give me the phone now."

Instead he chose to ignore me and turned the other way.

"As I was saying Mrs. Williams, I have a few ideas that you can shove u—"

"Blake!" I yelled before he could complete the sentence.

He again turned his back towards me and this time I lost it. "What the…?"

"Sorry terrible reception here." He continued. "So, as I was saying, in matters concerning your daughter you can…"

Before he could finish the sentence I jumped on his back and he staggered almost dropping the phone.

"What are you doing?" he yelled but I was too busy trying to balance on his back as well as make a grab for the phone.

I finally yanked the phone from his hand and almost fell off his back but he steadied me.

"Hi, mom."

I sounded breathless and completely flustered. I mean I was pretty sure some of the tourists took a picture of me thinking. I was some circus act leaping on a poor boys back and grabbing his phone.

"Darella? What's going on?" My mom's voice sounded sharp.

"You can't rule her life, she i—" I clamped my hand over Blake's mouth.

"Oh, nothing mom, some big circus troop in Rome… Ewww! Did you just spit on my hand?"

Blake didn't give a response instead yelled into the phone. "You lifeless b—"

"Mom, the connection is really bad!" I yelled before he could complete the sentence.

"Hen—" her voice said before it was cut by Blake yelling. "Your mom is a—"

"What on earth is going on?" My mom yelled.

"Shut up!" I yelled. "No, not you mom it's chaos here."

"He's going to meet you in Rome…" my mother said quickly. "Darella, whatever is happ—"

"Mrs. Williams please go take your big as—"

I yelped. "Gotta go." Before throwing the phone which hit the ground and went black.

For a minute the both of was staring at his now dead phone, with me still on his back.

"You just killed my phone!" He yelled childishly.

"You almost killed me!" I yelled back.

"Well it doesn't seem you are living much anyway…"

"Not this argument again." I groaned. "Why are you getting all huffy over it?"

Blake would have probably come up with an answer had it not been for a voice suddenly saying. "Dare?"

I looked up startled at the scrawny boy who just said my name. He was pale bespectacled and frankly looked slightly scared of me.

"And who are you?" Blake asked rudely.

At that moment I couldn't blame the boy for looking so confused and scared. I mean Blake was a pretty intimidating guy and it didn't help that I was still on Blake's back and he was supporting all hundred and twenty pounds of me easily as I simply stayed in my position looking shocked.

And then I recognize him.

"I-I'm Henry," he said unsurely. "D-Dare what's going on?"

"Yeah, Dare, what's going on?"

I could clearly here Blake's voice turning sharper. Even though I couldn't see his face, I knew his grey eyes had just become harder.

I carefully came down from his back and almost tripped and fell flat on my face but thankfully Blake managed to catch me in the last moment.

"Thanks." I muttered before turning my attention to the new arrival.

"Blake this Henry. Henry this is Blake."

Blake's eyes narrowed as he took in all five feet, five inches of Henry along with his sleek gelled brown hair and expensive shoes.

"Who is he?" Blake asked rather bluntly.

I was about to answer but Henry beat me to it. "Her future fiancé?"

Uh-oh.

CHAPTER ELEVEN

The silence was unnerving.

Blake stared at Henry, Henry stared at me and I prayed to every god there was to get me out of this situation.

"So my mother sent you?" I asked once more.

"Yes, she was worried about you." Henry replied. "She said that you had gotten yourself in quite a situation and I was in Greece anyway closing an account so I decided to drop by."

Something in his tone clearly didn't add up. It was shaky and unsure. I was most certain he was lying and it was blatantly obvious.

Blake clenched his fists. "Told you that your mother is a—"

I glared at him and he stopped.

"You know what I don't need this," he said getting up. "I'm going out, call me once you're done."

With that he stalked away.

"Your friend there is moody and quite hot too." Henry remarked nonchalantly.

I raised an eyebrow at his remark and he quickly corrected himself. "I mean for a boy. He's gay, right?"

That was when I started choking on my coffee.

"Are you alright?" Henry asked concerned.

I gave him a weak thumbs up. Then I noticed that Blake was sitting right behind Henry in the next booth looking slightly enraged.

So much for "*I can't take this anymore*".

"Well, if he was gay then I wouldn't have to listen to him rate every single girl who walked by us." I stated drily.

He rolled his eyes behind Henry and pointed at Henry and holds up a zero sign.

It was my turn to roll my eyes.

Yeah, life would be much simpler if he was gay. Then I would know for sure that I didn't have a shot with him.

"Oh, so he's straight?" Henry looked kind of disappointed. "Did anything happen between you two?"

Blake started to get up and I glared at him giving him the *shut-up-and-sit-down look.*

'No, Henry nothing happened." I said forcing a smile. "We are just friends."

"Which is why you were on his back?" He asked.

"That was a bit of an accident." I said carefully.

"I should sure hope so," he said and I tried to resist the urge to slap him. Behind him Blake holds up a tissue paper with "jerk" written on it.

For once I agreed with him completely.

"So..." I trailed off trying to find something to talk about. I wanted Blake to come back but god knew what Henry would go tell my mother if he got punched in the face and let's not forget the law suit that would follow.

"That's a really pretty blouse. It's from the summer collection of Burberry right?"

I looked down at my black top which was floral printed. I was wearing it with a knee length pleated skirt and my favourite pair of worn out Converse shoes which had been the only pair of shoes I had brought with me.

My mother didn't even know that I owned these pair of shoes and she would probably have a heart attack of she ever found out. In fact, come to think of it, these shoes were one of the only things in my wardrobe that I had picked out for myself everything else was my mom.

"I suppose so." I said.

Blake once again held up a tissue paper with "snob" written on it.

Once again I found myself agreeing with him.

"So you're not interested in fashion?" Henry asked.

"Not really, why are you?" I asked and he got a dreamy look on his face.

"Yes. I mean look at your top it's such a beauty to look at," he said. "The design is so flawless and the colors…"

He broke off at my baffled expression and quickly said. "I mean yeah suits and shoes."

Okay, that was weird.

This time Blake was holding up a tissue paper that said "gay."

I roll my eyes at his immature comment.

"So..."

Blake was still holding up the sign and pointing frantically at it. I couldn't believe that he was such a homophobe and I glared at him.

He then pointed to Henry's hair and I found myself looking at it. It was perfectly combed in place with a single curl jutting out like superman. It was a shiny brown with gold highlights and was much better maintained than my hair.

He had the exact same hairstyle when I was first introduced to him a few months back during a wedding during New Year's Eve. My parents had ditched me with him almost expecting me to kiss him at midnight. Thankfully, I was saved then but right now I had no other option.

He was about to say something, but Blake came and sat beside me almost throwing me off the sofa saying. "You're gay, aren't you?"

"Blake!"

"Please don't tell."

Henry and I said it both at once and I looked at him with wide-eyed shock. Blake had a triumphant smirk on his face while Henry's skin turned into a shade of pale yellow.

"Y-you're gay?" My voice was small and unsure.

He looked at me nodding. "Yes I am."

Blake smiled in a comforting way. "Hey, man there is nothing to feel bad about."

Hold it.

I was going to marry someone who is gay?

"Henry, how are we going to get married if you're gay?" My voice was shaky.

"I thought you were doing it to hide something, too," he said. "I mean with your…"

"Hold it!" I said. "You think I'm gay, too?"

He glanced at Blake and then looked back at me. "Aren't you?"

"Wha—"

I started to say but Blake interrupted me. "I don't blame you for thinking that. I mean she's been staying with me for the past week and she's not even blinked an eye towards me."

Well, he was right in a way. Whenever I looked at him I never blinked, but that was because I didn't look—I ogled. I honestly thought that he had noticed it. I mean when he came out of the shower in only a towel, I swear to god I drooled a bit.

Okay not a bit, a lot.

Like I was going to tell him that.

"But she does fangirl over Orlando Bloom like there is no tomorrow." Blake said. "She said, and I quote, I want my ova—"

"Hey, Blake," I said kicking his foot hard. "Too much information."

This was just embarrassing.

While I was watching TV, something very unladylike might have slipped from my mouth regarding Orlando Bloom and my ovaries.

Yeah. I said that out *loud.*

Blake laughed so hard that he fell off the bed along with our popcorn. I turned a deep shade of scarlet as he continued to laugh.

When he finally finished his laughing fit, he told me that it was fine. Guys won't admit it but they had a little man-crush on Orlando Bloom, too. After all he was a 9.2 out of 10.

"Okay, so then why are you going through with this?" Henry asked me looking a bit weirded out. "I can't possibly tell my parents that I'm gay."

"Why not?" Blake asked, his eyes flashing angrily. "I mean, are your parents that backwards or do they have their heads stuck up their asses that far that they cannot accept who you are?"

Poor Blake. He didn't understand just how bad the situation was but I did. Parents who had spent too much of their life obtaining the perfect image would tear down anything that would tarnish it, even their own kids.

I looked at Henry sympathetically. Before I used to think that he was a snob and jerk, but his situation was as bad as mine.

"Henry, I'll help you," I said softly. "I don't mind marrying you if that means it will keep your secret safe."

"What?"

I ignored Blake and continued looking at Henry who looked shocked. "I know how parents are and I understand your situation."

Henry looked at me stammering. "Y-you'll actually marry me even after you know?"

I nod earnestly. "Yup."

"You won't tell anyone?" he asked again.

"No," I said firmly. "It's not my secret to tell."

Henry looked so shell-shocked it was almost funny. I didn't know what made me say it, but it was true what I had said. There were plenty of worse people out there and Henry wasn't one of them. Besides it would be a win-win situation. Both Henry's and my parents would be happy.

Plus, I didn't want to find out what substitute my parents would find to Henry.

"Henry, isn't there someone you like?" Blake started.

Henry looked dazed. "Love, actually. There is this guy who is absolutely amazing."

I smiled. "That's brilliant."

Blake didn't give up though. "Don't you think that you should stand up for what you have?"

"I can't," he said, looking at me helplessly and then at Blake. "My parents will kill me."

"But love is worth fighting for…" Blake said a little too forcefully, "I can't believe how you, both of you are willing to give up everything just because your parents said so, it's flipping ridiculous."

He looks off into the distance his grey eyes stormy and angry.

"Henry," I said calmly. "Go to the person you love honestly and I promise to be your cover, okay. No matter how long it takes for you to tell your parents."

He stared at me dumbly. "You don't know me, why would you do this for me? You can easily blab to your parents and get out of this."

"I'm not that kind of person, in fact I'll prove it to you," I said, scooping his iPhone off the table.

I leaned forward and kissed him on the lips and clicked a picture simultaneously.

"There," I said handing the phone back to him. "You can send it to anyone you like I'm sure your parents will be happy. Maybe make the guy jealous?"

He looked at me and then stared at his phone like it was a piece of uranium in his hand. It should be, after all it was a picture of my first kiss and the best way of hiding his secret.

Blake was looking at me with an expression that said that he was trying to figure me out but he kept quiet this time and stared at Henry.

"So, tell me more about this guy." I said.

Henry's eyes immediately got brighter. "He is Indian. Tall, dark, and handsome sort."

I laughed. "That's amazing. Where did you guys meet?"

"In one of the boring accounts meetings. I'd gone to Greece as an excuse to see him."

I couldn't help but smiling. This was what love was about. Secret meetings, blushing at the very thought of a person. I felt sorry for Henry that he couldn't do it openly maybe someday he would have the guts to do it.

And I meant it, I would help him. Honestly speaking I'm pretty sure after this vacation my "love story" or more like the story of me pathetically pining over a guy, would come to an end but if I could help someone else make theirs come true I would honestly help them.

Henry's phone suddenly rang and he almost dropped it.

"It's your mother," he said shakily.

I sighed. "Go ahead give me the phone, I'll say everything is fine."

Henry looked at me with a weird expression before he picked up the phone.

"Hello, Mrs. Williams," he said politely into the phone. Next to me, Blake was completely rigid and his knuckles were white.

"Dare, you can't…" he started to say but I give him a "shhh" sign and he shut up.

"Yes, she's with me." Henry said. "Yes, I'll give it to her in a moment."

"Mrs. Williams I just wanted to inform you that I cannot marry Dare."

What the…?

"I just think that it's not fair since I'm gay and in love with a man," he said cheerfully. "Nice talking to you."

And he shut the phone.

I looked at him wide-eyed and in shock. Blake had a similar expression on his face but it was tinged with a slight smirk.

"Wow, I just did that,." Henry said, looking at his phone.

"You didn't have to do that," I said breathlessly. "I'll tell her that you were drunk or some—"

"It really is okay, Dare. I'm doing this for me. Honestly, I can't asked you to do something like that but the very fact that you were willing to let go of probably your entire life for me says that I can't be that big of a jerk and actually let you go through with it."

He glanced at Blake again who now had a full blown grin. "Besides, your friend here was right. Love is worth being brave for, and honestly, I'm sorry for being such a jerk to you. A part of me was hoping you would just cancel the wedding and I would have no choice but to come out."

"But your parents…" I trailed off before realising how stupid I was being.

"That was the bravest thing I've ever seen anyone do," I said finally.

"I agree," Blake said. "But that's the second bravest thing. Sorry man, a girl willing to marry you and ruin her own life just to help you out seemed a whole lot braver."

Henry nodded sincerely. "I agree, thank you so much Dare," he said pulling me into a tight hug. "Thank you for making me brave."

He then laughed and took the phone. "I have to go and say I love you, if you don't mind I'm going to keep the picture to you know make him jealous."

I laughed and gave him a big thumbs up. "Best of luck."

He then more or less ran out of the cafe tripping on his way and I couldn't help but smile.

Maybe one day I would be able to do what he did. Show up everyone and do what I wanted.

That day I knew exactly who I would run to… and it would most definitely be to Blake.

CHAPTER TWELVE

"Were you actually willing to marry him knowing that he loved another person?" Blake said looking at me curiously.

"Why not?" I shrugged. "That way at least one of us would have a happy ending."

He looked at me dumbly. "So you actually don't mind spending your life without loving anyone, being on your own."

At that point I wanted to throw my arms around Blake and tell him that these few days with him were enough to last me a lifetime but I didn't and I simply nodded.

"Yes, don't look so shocked. Not all of us have the guts to fight for love no matter how much we want to Blake. Some of us are just meant be supporting characters in the love story."

He rolled his eyes. "That's utter crap."

"Okay, Romeo." I said shrugging. "Now get up, I want to visit the Trevi fountain."

I looked outside and it was already getting dark. How long had we spent in this place?

He obliged and I found myself walking with him through the streets of Rome while he was desperately trying to figure out the map.

We had come to a joint censuses after last time that he would handle the directions.

We finally reached the fountain and it was crowded with tourists. There weren't that many but almost all of them were kissing and taking pictures.

I suddenly become really self-conscious.

"What Henry did…?" I said slowly "…I can never do."

He looked at me his grey eyes almost black in the dim light. "Here," he said, handing me a coin Make a wish."

I rolled my eyes. "This is so cliché."

He didn't say anything but closes his eyes and after a brief moment he tossed his coin into the fountain.

"Your turn."

"What should I wish for?" I asked. "Guts?"

"Eyes." Blake muttered sarcastically.

"What?" I asked him confused. He shook his head and gave me a small smile. "Just wish for something, Dare."

I closed my eyes and clutched the coin tightly in my closed fist. There were a lot of things I wanted to wish for, being brave, being loved being better at being me but one wish stood out very clearly.

I wish for this summer to last forever.

An impossible wish but the thing I wanted most.

I tossed my coin in the fountain and smiled as it sank to the bottom with thousands of other coins.

"So what did you wish for?" Blake asked looking curious.

I rolled my eyes. "Like I'm going to tell you Romeo."

He rolled his eyes. "Why Romeo?"

"Because you're all about true love and fighting for love and being brave for love and stuff." I said shrugging.

"Romeo was the biggest freaking wimp on the planet." Blake stated. "The guy knew how to love but he ran away when he lost that love. If you are brave enough to love, you should be brave enough to face the fact that you may lose it or have it slip out of your grasp in a matter of seconds."

I raised an eyebrow.

For the life of me I couldn't figure out what Blake Durham was made of. One minute he would rate girls like any normal pig of a guy would, and the other minute he would spout up deep and philosophical fact about true love that would leave my mouth hanging open.

"Don't you have anything to say like Romeo and Juliet were one of the greatest love stories written and how I could possibly say that?" He asked me and I shook my head.

"I don't think Shakespeare wrote Romeo and Juliet for the love story, Blake," I said. "I think it's to remind us that not all of us have happy endings. Even the people who find love."

"You, sir, are a ray of sunshine," he said and I started laughing.

"Well, what did you wish for?" I asked.

"Like I'm about to tell," he said walking closer to the fountain. "That would completely ruin my dark and mysterious aura."

I rolled my eyes. "Dark and mysterious? You're one haircut away from becoming the beloved TV show character strawberry shortcake."

"Really, strawberry shortcake?" he said pouting. "I thought if I would become a TV show character it would either Johnny Bravo or Popeye. I do a killer sailor impression."

He wiggled his eyebrow and said. "Aye, aye."

I found myself laughing. "One problem, *sailor man*, you can't swim."

He pouted like a little kid. "I hope you enjoyed crushing my hopes and dreams."

"Grow up." I said smiling.

We both laughed and settled into our usual comfortable silence.

"Wow! That was some day, huh?" I said after a while and he nodded.

"Next time you want a piggy back ride, please ask," he said. "Honestly it's awesome when a girl actually jumps on you but it's not so awesome when she is trying to scratch your face off."

"I was not trying to scratch your face off," I said giving him an offended look. "I was trying to snatch your phone."

He simply kept quiet and I realised something.

"Wow, I just realised that I had my first kiss today," I said. "And I don't even remember how it felt like."

Blake stopped on his tracks.

"That was your first kiss?" he asked. "And you just gave it away like that?"

I rolled my eyes. "You make it sound so dramatic."

"Umm, it's a big deal," he said. "I still remember my first kiss. I was fourteen and I had this really awkward date with a girl who was like two years older than me and she just kissed me out of the blue. I honestly saw fireworks."

"That's a riveting story," I said sarcastically.

"Bottom line is that you remember your first kiss," he said.

"Thanks but I…"

Before I can complete the sentence, he grabbed me by my waist and kissed me.

Blake had describe it perfectly, fireworks. It wasn't a really long one but I still felt it all the way till the tip of my toes. He was right, it was like fireworks. It lasted only for a moment, but that moment was so pretty and so beautiful that it didn't matter.

He finally pulled back and grinned. "A romantic kiss in front of the Trevi Fountain, now that's what a first kiss should be like. One you will remember."

He was right, it was certainly a memory that I would remember.

A memory that would last me forever.

CHAPTER THIRTEEN

"God, this place is freaking gorgeous." I said scanning the Boboli Gardens in Florence.

Blake nodded wordlessly, looking at the beautiful garden stretched out in front of us, lost in his own thoughts.

Blake has been like that the past two days since our kiss in the Trevi Fountain. At first, he was fine. But during our walk to the hotel, he became silent so suddenly.

I didn't know if I should be worried about him but I certainly didn't want to pry. Blake was quite secretive when it came to his own personal life. I was scared that if I crossed that line he would revert back to the cold withdrawn Blake he had been at first.

We did make small talk, but we didn't talk about the kiss. It was a silent agreement that he initiated because, well, he was just that kind of guy and it mustn't have meant anything.

I wish he wasn't the kind of guy who could make a kiss look so casual and so small because, for me, it was a big deal and he was pretty much ruining it for me.

But I knew, while the kiss would last for a lifetime in my memory, the trip wouldn't and so was my time with Blake. So I decided to be cheerful for the both of us and stop overthinking everything.

I kept babbling about random facts about Florence even though Blake's attention was barely on me.

"Any chance I can tap that?"

My face turned a nasty shade of scarlet as I heard a group of boys whistling at me.

I chose to ignore them and just look ahead and continue my speech about the history of Florence, but I was interrupted again.

"Those legs will look better wrapped around me now, won't they?"

This time Blake heard it and turned around, his grey eyes narrowed and his fist clenched.

The leader of the group, a boy with a cigarette in his hand which miraculously hadn't been caught, laughed. "I meant the girl, not you."

Blake started to move forward but I blocked his path.

"Totally not worth it." I said through gritted teeth.

"Someone scared?" The boy taunted. Blake took a step forward but I didn't budge and stood my ground, still blocking his way. "Eye for an eye makes the whole world blind."

He suddenly jerked backward at that as if I've electrocuted him by quoting Gandhi.

"What a little bitch."

I turn around and glared at the guy. "Shut up."

All five of them laughed and the boy with the cigarette blew smoke on my face. "What are you going to do about it? Spank me? Or tell your spineless friend to do it?"

He blew smoke on my face again and that's when I lost it.

I punched him.

At first, I didn't realize what I did but his cigarette dropped to the ground while he clutched his bloody nose shocked.

All five of them stared at me almost comically, most of them frozen trying to process in their tiny brains what just happened and that's when Blake started laughing.

The boys finally recovered and the one in front made a leap for me but Blake grabbed my hand pulling me out of the way. "Run. Run. Run."

And that's how I ended up laughing, stumbling through the Boboli gardens hand in hand with Blake.

We didn't stop until we lost them and I almost collapsed on the grassy ground.

"That was exhausting." I said, sitting down, wiping all the sweat off my forehead.

"So much for an eye for an eye," he said. I shrugged. We both held eye contact for a minute before laughing our heads off and collapsing on the grass like maniacs.

When we finally managed to stop, Blake told me, "That was some serious moves, Dare Williams."

"Got them all from Kung Fu Panda," I said earnestly and he grinned.

"Up is my favorite animated movie." Blake uttered, smiling faintly. "Whenever my sister and I would watch it, she'd start crying in no more than the first ten minutes."

"Really?" I asked, realizing that this is the first time he has ever spoken about his family. "I started in the first five and didn't stop until after the credits and I wish I was exaggerating."

"I always thought that you would be The Notebook kind of girl," he said and I shake my head.

"Nope. I don't get the big deal really," I said. "Hayley has watched it like a billion times and I still don't get what's the big deal about that movie."

"Tell that to my mom and sister," he said settling down on the grass. "They would literally camp out in front of our telly with a huge bowl of popcorn and a whole box of tissues. I tried watching it once and got bored in like two seconds. I guess my sister did too because she spent the rest of the movie drawing stuff on my face while I was asleep"

I smiled realizing that, despite how hard and tough Blake may be, he had this big soft spot for his family.

"She would have loved this place, Dare," he said softly, looking up at the sky. "She was always a history nut and this place has history coming out of its ears."

"What's her name?" I asked in a whisper, lying down next to him.

"Jenna," he replied with a faint smile. "She hated her name."

The name on the planner.

"What happened to her?" I said, trying to keep my voice as gentle as possible.

His head whipped to my direction so fast that I heard the whooshing of the wind. "How did you know?"

I turned towards him. "Her name's written in your planner."

For a second, I think I crossed the line but he simply sighed.

"It was hers," he said after sometime. "Not mine. When she…"

He was silent for some time. "She had leukemia. She was diagnosed when she was fourteen, so she made this list of all the places she wanted to visit but she…" he paused and swallowed, "died before she could see the whole of Italy."

I didn't say anything for some time trying to take in what he said.

"She gave me this planner with all the name of the places in Italy she still wanted to go to and asked me to fill it in for her," he said faintly.

I wanted to say I'm sorry but that didn't even begin to cover what he must be going through.

"I think that wherever she might be right now, she must be happy." I said after some time.

He looked at me, his grey eyes calculating. "How do you know?"

His tone wasn't not accusing or demanding. He was simply curious.

I rolled over so I was facing him. His face was merely inches from me. His grey eyes were wide and he is looked at me with an expression that was part cautious and part curious.

"She was loved." I said simply. "She died knowing you loved her and I think that's the best way to die."

"She didn't deserve to die, loved or not," he said bitterly.

I settled back on the grass, looking up at the sky which started to turn dark.

"It's a myth that bad things happen only to bad people," I said quoting what he had said to me a few days back.

"That's what she used to say," he said. "I still think its bullshit."

"No one wants to die," I said after sometime. "But when they do,

I think the best way to go is to know that you were loved. When you die knowing you will be missed, not in a sad way, but a happy way. Like people recalling and laughing at the way your laugh was so weird or your annoying habit of blabbering on without a care. I think that's the best way to come to terms with something we have no control over."

He didn't reply.

"Dying knowing you've been loved is something not everyone is lucky enough to experience," I said, looking at the moon that had faintly appeared in the sky.

We stayed quiet for some time and I finally got up, brushing the grass of my shorts.

"We should get going, they will probably start closing the gates soon," I said.

"Hey Dare?" he said.

"Yeah?" I said not looking at him.

"You know that you are one of them, right?" he said stumbling a bit. "One of those people who will die being loved."

I gave Blake a faint smile and a kiss on the cheek. "I know."

CHAPTER FOURTEEN

"After her death, I just withdrew," he said in the car. "I left, putting college on hold, and just went away. My parents have always been well off so I travelled, everywhere but there."

"Why now?" I asked. "Why choose now to come to Italy?"

He shrugged. "I don't know," he answered honestly. "It just felt right."

"Dave thinks that you've come here with your friends," I said slowly.

He gave me a faint smile. "That's what my parents think, that I'm partying and having the time of my life. All I'm really doing is visiting all the places my sister went," he continued. "I'm trying desperately to move on, trying to see what she did."

"And did you?" I asked.

He turned towards me and gave me a slight smile. "Yeah. Yeah I think I did."

"Verona."

"Romeo and Juliet," I said.

"I think that's incredibly unfair," he stated. "It's such a beautiful place and all people can think about is Romeo and Juliet."

I rolled my eyes. "You really don't like that story do you?"

"I used to think it was accurate, once upon a time," he said. "That love is synonymous with tragedy and heartbreak."

"Really?" I said acting surprised. "Blake Durham used to be a non-believer."

He rolled his eyes. "Ha-ha. Very funny."

I shrugged. "I know. I'm hilarious."

He shook his head and walked on.

"So what made you change your mind and go all pro-love?" I asked. He took out a letter from his pocket. It was crumpled but it was still intact in its envelope

"My sister gave this to me," he said after some time. "It took me a while to figure out what she was saying but now that I have, it's time to let go of it, let go of her."

We walked in silence for some time.

"We're here!" he finally announced, looking at the beautiful mansion in front of us. "Juliet's house."

I looked at the structure in astonishment. It was beautiful. It's exactly where you would imagine a Shakespearean love story would take place.

It was night time and the place was beautifully lit up with fairy lights hung everywhere. I could actually picture the ball, one with masks, lights, and aristocrats all coming together underneath the stars to give rise to the beginnings of the greatest love story ever told.

"Woah!"

"Woah!" was exactly how to describe it. Hundreds of letters, post its, writings all of them plastering the wall. No two letters were alike. Someone had posted a bright pink paper right next to an old yellowing envelope that seemed to look like something that Juliet herself had written.

That's how love was, understood and expressed in so many ways. But one thing is common. All forms of love hopes of the happy ending that Juliet never got.

I absent mindedly traced my hand over the large heart drawn with *Andrew loves Mara* written on it.

Blake twisted a letter in his hand, and after a moment of hesitation, he walked ahead and placed the letter in a small crevice in the wall. He stood there again trying to figure out what to do and turned towards me for a fraction of a second before stepping away from the wall.

"Do you think even half of the relationships on this wall made it?" I asked, not wanting to pry about the letter.

"Yeah, I think actually all of them did in their own way," he said slowly.

I looked at him surprised at his answer. "What do you mean?"

He smiled broadly as if he just realized something.

"Love is something that isn't meant to last forever. It's a memory more than anything, a part of you that makes you want to be a better person," he said finally. "But even if the love fades, the memory of it doesn't. And that's what makes each of these relationships special. It doesn't matter if two people are no longer together. When they stuck their letter here or wrote their names in a heart, they were in love and that memory of being in love will last them a lifetime."

"Love is there to find only for those who are brave enough to go and search for it, Blake." I said dryly. "Learning from Juliet, it's best to just keep to yourself."

"It's not her fault that Romeo was a complete idiot," he said rolling his eyes.

"But Romeo was extraordinary, he was…"

"Don't you get it yet Dare?" he said. "It's never the person you fall in love with who is extraordinary, its love that's extraordinary. The way you feel about that person is what makes even the most ordinary of people special."

He paused and then added, "Even if Romeo loved or not, he's still was still lame."

"Oh, I'm sorry not everyone is a British rendition of Prince Charming who can make you fall in love with them in no time at all." I said sarcastically. Blake grinned.

"Aha!" he exclaimed. "And there it is, finally!"

I quirked an eyebrow.

"And there we have it, admittance." He laughed. "A bit longer than I expec—"

"What on earth are you talking about?"

"How long does it take for you to admit that I am insanely charming?" he answered.

I laughed out loud. Insanely charming didn't even begin to cover it but I wasn't going to tell him that.

"I thought you heard me saying that in my sleep already," I said smirking.

He scratched the back of his head sheepishly. "Yeah, I may have lied about that."

I narrowed my eyes.

"Don't blame me. You were really hard to figure out and you didn't make it any easier that I was so head over heels in love with you."

I froze in my spot and he smirked.

"There, I said it," he said triumphantly. "I am in love with you Dare Williams."

The color of my face completely drained and for a second, I thought it was a joke, a horrible joke the universe was doing to me.

"Blake." My voice came out weak and strangled. "Don't do this, please don't."

His face fell. "Why? Are you telling me that you don't…?"

"Of course, I do," I whispered. "I fell the minute you brought me the hazelnut ice cream in Pompeii. But you can't do this to me, not now. Not when I'm finally coming to terms…"

I stop looking at his blank guarded expression.

"You remember what you told me?" I asked him as he looked away from me. "You told me that you were finally going to go back and meet your parents… that you were going to follow your dreams and pursue becoming a writer. This summer wasn't meant to last forever, Blake, and I have to face reality."

"You're seriously not considering going back and getting your life dictated by your parents, are you?" he said.

I gave him a small smile. "Yes, but this time I'll do it on my own terms."

"What if you don't have to, Dare?" he said, his eyes shining brightly. "Come with me. Live your life."

I put my hands around him and smiled at him, a genuine big one, nothing held back. "I really do love you, Blake Durham."

"I fell in love with you the minute you tripped and almost took me down with you in Caserta," he said, slowly taking the hair out of my eyes. "I knew I was in love with you when I almost drowned to prove my point in Amalfi. I love you, Dare Williams, and it's because of you that I finally see what my sister was saying. It's because of you that I see the beauty of love. No matter what you choose, I will always love you."

I didn't know when I started tearing up. It was a strange thing crying, crying when you weren't sad but when you were so happy that your heart felt like it was going to burst.

He put his arm around my waist and looked up at the stars. "It is not in the stars to hold our destiny but in ourselves."

I laughed, looking at the stars with him. "Shakespeare."

His gaze turned towards me and I realized that he was right. Falling in love even just once is worth all the pain and all the fear. For once I understood why Juliet did what she did, why Hayley and Dave were always taking pictures with each other and why Henry defied his parents just so that he could write his own love story.

Because love is worth it and in the end, it's all you leave behind when you die.

The relationship may die, the memories may fade, but love lasts forever.

"I will never stop loving you," I whispered and that was when he kissed me.

The ending of this book is for you to decide. Whether I moved on with life braver, stronger, and with nothing but the memory of Blake and how much he loved me and how he taught me to be fearless.

Maybe I finally took control of my life and showed my parents that my life was to be lived on my own terms.

Maybe I ran away with him, lived the rest of my life falling in love with him in a new way each day.

Or maybe I got all of them. Maybe I got none of them.

But the one thing that I could tell you was that my wish came true. The summer did last forever because I learned to be brave, I learned to fall in love, and more than anything else, I learned that everyone has something to fight for.

So for all those out there hoping for a happy ending, it does exist. For all those who have stopped believing in love and are so caught up in the pain, don't give up on your happy ending. Everyone gets their happy ending. Maybe not always in the way we want but in a way that only we can understand.

And I understood, because right there below the stars next to Juliet's house, where one of the greatest love stories took place, Blake gave me the happy ending that Shakespeare never wrote for Juliet.

A happy ending that lasted me a lifetime.

Epilogue

Dear Blake,

Cheer up. Yeah, you know it's bad when the girl with leukemia is telling you to cheer up. Honestly, you're being a kill joy and that's my job, not yours. So after reading this letter, promise me something. Smile and throw this letter away.

With the way things are going, I'm not going to be able to see Italy and that's okay because I want you to see it for me. I want you to fall in love with that place like I fell in love with this world. Remember, the brightest of flames burn for the shortest time.

I know this has been hard for you, Blake. After all, in your seventeen years of life, your top priority has been me. Thank you for that. Honestly, if I was standing at the edge of a cliff, I'd have already fallen off if it weren't for you.

I still remember the day I was diagnosed and told that I had barely two years to live you. You were going out with Marcia Goldman then. You broke up with her on that very same day and didn't date anyone after. I didn't understand why at first but now I do.

Blake you put up a tough guy act. You try to be brave on the outside but you are terrified all the time of losing someone you love. And when you came to accept that you were going to lose me, you just decided not to love anymore. After all, if you don't love anymore then no way you get hurt anymore, right?

Well, that's complete and utter crap, big brother. Love makes us brave. It makes us reckless, passionate, and more than anything, it gives us a reason to live and a reason to die. It opens our eyes and then gives us a reason to close them so we can dream.

Your love has taught me to be brave, Blake and now, I'm telling you to be brave. I'm telling you to not to be afraid of falling in love. Go to Italy and meet a girl. Better yet, take a girl on a road trip with you to Italy. After all, the great Robert Frost is right. You shouldn't go on road trips with someone you don't love.

Fall in love, Blake. Maybe give Marcia another shot. I don't know, I don't care. Honestly, I have a lot of things on my mind and I can't be worried about you dying sad and alone with forty cats, I just can't.

I love you, Blake. Nothing will change that even if you lose me. I hope you know that. I promise to haunt your ass till your ninety years old with a bajillion grand kids and great grand kids, out of which at least a hundred should be named Jenna.

I'm giving you my planner, the one I was going to take to Italy, so that you can write your story in it and it better be a love story. All I ask you to do is learn to fall in love again and understand that it is love that makes us strongest at our weakest moments.

Blake, if someone you love dies, I'm sure they'll die knowing that they were loved totally and completely by you.

You gave me the best thing possible. You never gave up on me and loved me till the end and I hope you give someone else the chance to do the same for you. I hope you give someone else a chance to be a part of your happy ending like you were a part of mine.

Love,
Your amazing sister Jenna

P.S: On second thought, do not name them Jenna because let's face it, it's a pathetic name. Name them something awesome for my sake like Princess Leia or something.

P.P.S: Give mom and dad a call once in a while, will you? They worry.

P.P.P.S: I love you, always.

Dear Jenna,

I know it's stupid to write to you. I've tried many times but I've failed because I was so afraid that I only had one shot at it. I thought nothing was good enough.

But I finally found something important to tell you: You were right. I know, wherever you are, you are probably gloating and saying I told you so.

But the thing is, I always knew you were right but I wasn't ready to admit it.

I do have a hero complex. I think that it's up to me to try to save everyone and when you went, I realized just how out of our control our lives really were.

I was lost for two years and then I met her. Granted, our first meeting wasn't the best and I ended up losing your planner. I was about to lose it, thinking that this was the universe's way of telling me that I was being stupid but then by the weirdest of coincidences, she found me again and gave me your planner.

If I hadn't been so dense, I would have probably understood then that it was your weird way of telling me that she was the one. But I am your brother, so of course I was oblivious.

I didn't like her that much really, she seemed like one of those whiny girls who could only think of herself. But then you must have been looking out for me because we ended up getting stuck together.

Thank all the gods we did, because this girl... Jenna, she is something else. She is brave, she is funny, she is smart, and most of all, she is selfless. I fell in love with her so fast and so hard that I didn't have time to blink or breathe.

In her, I saw everything you were trying to tell me. Love, hope and courage. All this time, I thought that I wouldn't be able to go on but I can and I will. Not because you asked me to but because I finally understand why I should.

She is beautiful, Jenna, everything I could have wanted and I'm sure that you would love her, but as usual I don't have the guts to tell her.

I'm going to tell her tomorrow even though it's the last day of our trip and I'm going to let go of this letter by putting it on Juliet's wall, I think you'll like that won't you?

I'll get my happy ending sis don't worry I won't end up with 40 cats I'm more of a dog person.

Love,
Blake

P.S: I gave it a shot with Marcia and let's just say that it didn't work out.

P.P.S: kill joy? Please I exude charm.

P.P.P.S: You were right. You should never go on road trips with people you don't love. Love you, always.

I looked up from the letter Blake sent me, wiping the tears out of my eyes. The stupid guy actually photocopied all those letters and kept them.

I shook my head trying to suppress a grin. *That's cheating, Blake.*

I finally took the last of the contents out of the envelope. It's a simple post card with exactly six words written on it in Blake's neat handwriting, six words that made me run up the stairs to get ready to set out on my newest adventure.

Just six words.

So what if Paris is overrated?

Fine

OLIVIA HARVARD

handcuffs, kisses and awkward situations

One

If you have managed to claw your way to your last year of high school, I congratulate you. I really do. Not only is there the expectation that you have to provide a minimum number of hours per subject to study, but there are other expectations, too. Some of them are unspoken, like the fact that you're supposed to have kissed someone by the time you finish high school, or at *least* have been in a relationship. Because even though it isn't a written rule, the student body expects you to have completed it by the time you step up and take your graduation certificate. Other expectations are more vocal.

Like how you're supposed to demonstrate a particular level of maturity because you're suddenly given so much more freedom and opportunities. But when you're seventeen and still have to have a teacher's signature to go to the bathroom, it's arguably difficult. When you have to have permission to wash your hands, how does society expect you to decide what you want to do with your life?

Maybe it's the stress of graduating. Maybe it's the inner child in all of us, demanding release. Maybe it's all the expectations being thrown at us. Either way, the graduating students of Gregory High were definitely not acting like the mature and responsible individuals we were expected to be. "Would you rate his butt a seven or an eight?" Mel whispered.

Our school had been having huge career expositions for all graduating students, just to give us an idea of what our future options were. University professors and highly trained experts from various disciplines presented us with basic information on different courses. The lecture we were attending was hosted by the local police department. The two guys doing most of the talking looked like walking donuts, but at least they had brought along an undeniably fit rookie. “I don’t know,” I said as I squinted and leaned forward to get a clearer view. “His left butt cheek looks bigger than the right one.”

Mel’s jade green eyes widened as she leaned forward. “Hey, you’re right.”

Continuing our brilliant discourse on uneven butt cheeks, we compared it with other various human body parts. Before we knew it, the boring speech about Australian legislation and upholding the law seemed distant as we got lost in our own giggles.

“Officer Brandy, I think Miss Montgomery just volunteered for the demonstration.”

Realising I had sunk half way down to the floor in my own laughter, I straightened in my seat, eyes wide. “What?”

Mrs. Coleman was this cranky, old woman, who allegedly had voodoo dolls stuffed in her teacher's pigeon hole. Her dull grey eyes seemed to taunt me with mocking satisfaction as she nodded towards the stage. Thin lips curled into a wicked grin as I grumbled something in gibberish and trudged onto the stage.

I stood between the officers and waited for further instructions. They both smelled like strong coffee and being so close up, I could see a collection of sprinkles on one of the policemen’s moustache. My eyes fell down to his chest and caught sight of his golden name tag. His name was Officer Brandy.

“And we need one more volunteer.” His deep, booming voice echoed through the large space of the auditorium.

Instantly, everyone tried not to make eye contact. Being up on the podium meant each and every student was exposed to my examination. Guys kept their gazes anywhere but in the direction of the supervising students; up at the ceiling, down at their shoes, across to their friends. The girls had the same idea, hiding behind curtains of hair or suddenly finding an interest in their pleated skirts.

“I think Ryder Collins is interested.” The icy tone of Mrs. Coleman sliced through the tension.

At the start of high school, Ryder Collins’ popularity came with his varsity jacket, the same way girls got their popularity from their bras. And now that I think about it, when you’re twelve and just started high school, I’m not particularly sure how ‘cool’ you could get. At first, I didn’t think it would affect our friendship. But after three months of being on the footy team, he decided to use his position to hoist himself up on the highest possible level of the social ladder. He’d been bathing in fame ever since, while I had been trying to avoid the smallest attentions.

Ryder tossed a filthy look of disgust to his friends, got up and walked towards the stage. He was one of the very few male students that could pull off his uniform. Who would have known clip-on ties and pinstripe trousers could look good on someone under twenty?

I’d like to think that I bloomed in high school too, that I developed into a sophisticated and beautiful woman. But really, I was just as awkward and average as I was when I first started. It was completely infuriating because Ryder was poster boy material. This only added to the uncomfortable tension between us.

“Great,” Officer Brandy announced, clapping his meaty hands. “Now, as I was saying, the local police department has designed a new pair of handcuffs. They’re made out of metal that is up to three times stronger than the original material, and as you can see, has thicker links.”

I watched as he held up the handcuffs and the group of students eyed it in surprising curiosity. He had managed to capture the attention of the class as the jaws of the open cuffs dangled from his fingertips. Thinking it was stupid that everyone was so mesmerised by a pair of handcuffs. I snorted. Ryder must have had the same thoughts because he made an unattractive sound of dissatisfaction, too.

"This particular pair of handcuffs was designed for our plus-sized criminals, so it has more links," he continued, sliding his thick fingers down the long chain. The additional five links were hardly impressive, but by the way Officer Brandy was admiring them, you'd think they were solid gold. "The great thing about these new and improved cuffs is that they're just like houses. Only one key fits per pair. Now, this is only a prototype, so we're extremely fortunate to have the opportunity to feature it on this particular demonstration."

Excited murmurs came from a few members of the audience. Even Mel looked mildly interested. But then I realised she was only excited because Officer Brandy was now circling the stage. Before I could figure out what he was doing, he grabbed hold of my right wrist and snapped on a handcuff. The metal was warm from his hold as it clicked into place.

"What are you *doing*?" I asked, wide eyed.

Mrs. Coleman instantly scolded me for addressing a policeman in such an accusing manner. But I could hardly concentrate on what she was saying, because Officer Brandy had secured the other handcuff around Ryder's left wrist. Panic washed over me, drowning me in complete terror. I looked down at the piece of silver that connected us together and directed my gaze to meet Ryder's faded blue eyes. He looked just about as freaked out as I did.

"Garret, can you please grab the hammer?" Officer Brandy asked as he gently steered us towards a table. "Kids, place your hands on the table."

“We’re going to die,” I whispered, all sorts of terrible thoughts running through my mind. My stomach tightened to a squeeze and a bitter taste formed in my mouth.

When the hammer was in Officer Brandy’s hands, the audience seemed to be holding its collective breath as he lifted the tool into the air. When he slammed the hammer down against the woodwork table with force, a loud, sharp bang of impact echoed through the room like a gunshot. It scared me so much that my heart could have just fallen straight out of my butt. To emphasise his point, Officer Brandy continued to beat the hell out of the metal links that joined Ryder and I together.

After another ten seconds of deafening hits, he placed the hammer down with a clatter and held up the undamaged chain. Impressed claps and a couple of cheers erupted from the students. Even Ryder’s entourage seemed pretty impressed and didn’t bother to conceal their interest behind their cool expressions. Admittedly, if I weren’t contributing to the demonstration, I probably would have been attentive too, because other than the police, the most exciting thing that had ever happened in these career talks was when the science department from the local university made elephant toothpaste. It was something we were all shown in year seven, but that didn’t make it any less entertaining.

The bell rang not long after; it was the sweet chime of freedom singing into my ears. As the teachers stood to keep the students tame and explain further instructions, Officer Brandy gave us a grin.

“Thanks for helping out with the demonstration, kids,” he said, grabbing his foam cup of coffee and taking a quick drink.

Ryder, obviously getting impatient, held up his wrist, and the chain that bound us yanked my hand up with his. “Can we please go now?”

Officer Brandy lowered the cup from his lips and made a sound of agreement. He placed the cup back onto the table and fumbled around in his pockets. All his pockets. His bushy brows knitted together as he patted himself down and each time he reached in and came out empty handed, my stomach squeezed in both irritation and panic. "Garret, do you have the key?" he called, looking over at his partner. Garret, who had been talking with a few eager students, turned. Shaking his head, he answered, "You had them with you."

Officer Brandy nodded in agreement. "That's what I thought. Hey, Drew, have you seen the key?"

The rookie policeman shook his head as he strode towards us, hands digging into his pockets. "No, Sir."

When Brandy turned to us, he gave us a tight smile. I think it was meant to be reassuring but the way his lips curled, said otherwise. I suddenly felt light headed, my knees about to give way. He didn't have to say anything. His face said it all.

Officer Brandy had lost the key.

If you enjoyed this sample then look for:

Handcuffs, Kisses and Awkward Situations in Amazon

Other books you might enjoy:

Marriage by Law

N.K. Pockett

"Cute and funny read. You will just breeze through it."

Get it on Amazon!

Dragon of Legend: Destiny

Angelika Meyer

“Full of vivid images that pull you into a humorous, yet suspenseful story.”

Get it on Amazon!

Acknowledgement

I'd like to thank my friends, my family and my readers, who've supported me and encouraged me to no extent. Without them this book would simply be a jumble of words strung together.

A big thank you to BLVNP, for taking a chance on this book and publishing it. It's absolutely mind-blowing that they actually believed in this book more than I did and gave me the opportunity to share it with the world.

Last but not the least, a thank you to Dare and Blake for being such an outstanding characters who've shown me how to be brave, how to be happy and how to fall in love.

About the Author

Nylla Camphry is a sixteen-year-old author who loves reading books and writing. She started writing when she was thirteen and hasn't stopped since. Her book *Road Trip to Love* won the Watty Award in the online writing community, Wattpad.

Her other hobbies include listening to music, dancing, and singing. Her favourite subject is Computer Science and she hopes to become a Software Programmer one day.

CPSIA information can be obtained
at www.ICGtesting.com
Printed in the USA
LVOW04s0414270616
494235LV00029B/569/P